WHAT BOOKS PRESS

AN IMPRINT OF

THE GLASS TABLE

COLLECTIVE

LOS ANGELES

NO ONE DIES
IN PALMYRA OHIO

NO ONE DIES
IN PALMYRA OHIO

HENRY ELIZABETH CHRISTOPHER

LOS ANGELES

Library of Congress Cataloging-in-Publication Data

Names: Christopher, Henry Elizabeth, author.
Title: No one dies in Palmyra Ohio / Henry Elizabeth Christopher.
Description: Los Angeles : What Books Press, [2022] | Summary: "In a small
    town where the dead rise, a religious leader battles with his Christian
    faith and his love for those who love him"-- Provided by publisher.
Identifiers: LCCN 2022021296 | ISBN 9780996227681 (trade paperback)
Subjects: LCGFT: Novels.
Classification: LCC PS3603.H7636 N6 2022 | DDC 813/.6--dc23/eng/20220509
LC record available at https://lccn.loc.gov/2022021296

Cover art: Gronk, *Untitled*, mixed media on paper, 2021
Book design by Ash Good, www.ashgood.com

What Books Press
363 South Topanga Canyon Boulevard
Topanga, CA 90290

WHATBOOKSPRESS.COM

for John Ballenger

NO ONE DIES IN PALMYRA OHIO

AT THE BEGINNING of the world he remembered the tang of oil. It was all god's pieces clicking mechanically into place the gears the cores the plugs the shifting corkscrew diadems laser particles smaller than molecules the things that make molecules happen. When they all came together they sang a harmony of unimaginable longing and the longing when he pressed his nose deep into the dream of it tasted like motor oil which he knew the taste of from four years old his Old Father holding him down in the backyard strong hand on his arm a spoonful of oil now this will handle your proclivities son.

The Father had another dream recurrently of leaving his soul's body in bed and exploring the earth without it. In this dream he felt his essence pull into three distinct pieces and he went with the piece that was unconditionally him above great waters. This dream also took place before all creation. Now and then the dream progressed so that this piece of him rose through a veil of mist into an unmade cosmos and while he was there the sun formed behind him and he floated backwards into it until the skin of the sun enveloped him. In this place he did not burn or hurt for he had no blood or bone to worry about. He merely turned as a tadpole does in its egg. He slept the rest of his night in a gas giant.

This morning the third Saturday of the month of June the girl and the man held a conversation in the Father's study about biology. The girl's biology was such that she could not die. The man tried to explain this to her. He was a young coroner from the closest city over. He used his hands to articulate himself big broad gestures with these dainty hands skin so smooth the Father could see light reflecting from the perfect planes of his knuckles.

The girl was agitated. She wanted to die. She rented the attic in the blue farmhouse across the street was only seventeen years old and had wanted to die for the entirety of her life so far as she could tell.

It occurred to the Father it might just be this place. Palmyra. He shared a deep look with the Coroner that meant he knew.

What do you know about Shannon Wells the Coroner asked him this question later in bed wiping sweat from his high cheekbone no air conditioning in the house barely any electricity so to speak and nearly the height of summer. Ick. The Father felt bad about this but his late mother's window unit made a rattling hissing cranking noise when switched on for more than a minute at the wrong angle and anyway it was the Coroner's choice to stay the night here and not at his apartment in Cincinnati or a motel between here and there or something. Folks would get suspicious after a while he suspected and all for the simple matter of an air conditioner.

The Father thought about the question a moment then I don't know nothing about Shannon Wells he decided referring to the girl by first and last name making her proximate though in many ways they were already so proximate he felt her heart pulling on the valves of his each time they opened and shut.

The Coroner sat up in bed. When he sat up the sheets fell off his shoulders and uncovered suddenly the pitch and yaw of his back split silver in the country moonlight coming in from the open window. The Father reaching out thumbed over the lower vertebrae of his spine. How do you think this ends he whispered fearfully and the Coroner replied I guess Shannon dies and the Father said back I guess.

The place staggered itself out over the county line making switchbacks trying to decide which side it would fall on whose jurisdiction whose taxes this or that. A green metal sign stuck on a piece of rebar marked it from the state route as a place not worth stopping at but a place with a name nonetheless. Palmyra. Who had given it that name no one knew. Better than the place called Gray five or so miles as the crow flies which meant hiking through the corn fields so really it was farther than that.

It wasn't featureless but liked to be. It liked to claim it was almost nothing. But even vacuousness was a feature saying look at me look at me I'm lonely. I'm so so lonely and where has everyone gone that said they would populate me and make me plenty the earth the soil god's green America and still I remain waiting for filling god damn you.

Perhaps the land of the place wouldn't take the lord's name in vain. The place was a Christian place and the land Christian land. Grown up in the blood and sperm of Christ. The Father's father was the Old Father before him and his Father before him. A whole line of Fathers for Palmyra. The chapel being one of the few features the place possessed brick and white vinyl siding and a few small windows wearing a steeple like the embarrassed participant of a birthday party gone on a few hours past late and when days were cloudy and they often were it blended right into the background. Well good the Father thought that's one less impression he had to worry about.

Other than the chapel there was the blue farmhouse on the other side of the state route a few hodgepodge bungalows like the Father's set squat into the hills a lot of cornfields which turned to soy on rest years known in the Old Father's time as sabbath years and behind the Father's row of bungalows an amoebic oval of lake flat glassy and having nothing to do with absolutely anybody barely giving up any fish though it's not that no one tried to make a hobby of it despite difficulty. Minnows and mollies flourished in the reedy sidelines of the lake. Too small to get a hook in. Turtles occasionally vacationed on the shore dug eggs into the dirt to get them gobbled up by neighborhood dogs. Wild turkeys came around briefly until somebody with a shotgun shot and ate them. Mostly it was the migrants that came and stayed for a while the mallards and geese with wimple-feathered hairy children the stray dogs the stray shell casings the stray people Shannon.

Staring out his back window the Father wanted every day to

gather the circumference and content of the lake up in his two arms
feel how sweaty cold it was squeeze the life from it weep into its small
small heart.

The Coroner was up before sunrise but the Father was up earlier.
They met in the kitchen near the long window over the sink and part
of the counter with all the lake glittering in it and the top corner of
the Father's hen house. The Coroner poured himself a glass of water
from the tap offered one to the Father but the Father insisted he wasn't
thirsty he had all the water he needed thanks.

What we can say with certainty really the only thing we can say
with certainty is that these results can't be scientifically duplicated said
the Coroner by all accounts they're unexplainable have you ever heard
of Redi's jars. The Father said no but it sounded familiar and wasn't it
a little cold this morning when he wanted so to be warm. The Coroner
said *omne vivum ex vivo* so it should be inferred that all warmth comes
from warmth. He finished his water sat on the counter and they
watched the sun come up over the lake together then the Coroner
retrieved his clothes from under the bed dressed quietly and left for his
apartment two hours southwest.

Knotted golden bun piled on the back of her skull. This was to keep
her hair from her face. She worked most often stooped down and it
bothered her hairs in her eyes but why bother cutting it. Shannon
stepped from the Father's house in the evening large boyish hands
gripped tight and adamantly around nothing fingernails pressed deep
into the fatty heels of her palms. Already there were neighbors stationed
on their porches to stare at her. She yanked up her socks and started
across the road to the blue farmhouse.

A small woman greeted her in the kitchen. How are you dear. I'm
just fine. What did he want from you. He didn't want anything at all but
for that city kid to tell me things I already known. You're okay though.
I'm fine. She went up two flights of stairs to the attic to her room.

Her room. Exposed wooden floors angled roofbeams a chair
brought up from the landlady's garden shed single torn cushion crushed

onto the seat with yellow floral pattern may have once been white floral pattern couldn't it. Coffee table with empty cracked fish tank used to hold various insects for short-term observation a fist-sized rock on the mesh lid. The twin mattress smashed on her floor lumpy from age mostly not used in favor of the chair. Thumbtack in wall. Between thumbtack and wall her collection of suicide notes given back to her by their recipients posthumously. She would say post-humorously ha ha. She used to write those now really there was no point everything had been written out a hundred thousand times already. Tattered wool blanket with a big hole in the bottom for her foot to poke out on hot nights like the ones happening lately. Height of summer god it was wasn't it. Circular attic window. Just like in the movies. Opened all the time letting air in and rain and insects and only god knew what else.

The next morning Shannon went down from her room in her undergarments and found the landlord making breakfast and the Father sitting hands folded at the dining room table looking apologetic. He always looked apologetic on Sundays. A specific way his forehead pressed his eyebrows down his wiry lips compressed though he was middle-aged she knew he would develop permanent old man wrinkles soon like how her teachers sometimes used to tell her if you blow your nose wiping up you'll get a big crease in it after a while. So you'd better not do that. She told this to the Father and he looked even more apologetic. I don't know if that's true he said but if it is that's terrifying. She shrugged.

They tell kids anything nowadays said the landlady. She was the Father's age exactly they'd used to be married but not anymore for some reason. Shannon guessed she knew why but no one else did so she kept shut up about it. Smell of wet flour and blueberries flourished as the landlady slopped a spoonful of pancake batter onto the griddle.

Shannon Wells kicked the Father under the table. She barely spit her words out what are you doing here man I'm fine. He shrugged. I'm not doing anything today until service do you want to walk the lake with me. You could've just gone and done it on your own. You ought to know how it is. Yeah I guess so.

She guessed she did know but she wasn't afraid of anything which was a big difference between the Father and her. It was a wonder he wasn't scared of the landlady. She had a deference to her that could tempt fear at times especially when Shannon Wells was late for payments of five dollars a month on the attic or late for breakfast or late doing dishes on Wednesday evenings after community dinners. She did love the Father and always had in the strictest specific sense but let him stay for pancakes anyway even put extra blueberries in his because she knew he liked that. And the Father said thank you Edna very much and she said quietly don't mention it he still loved her a little bit unspecifically and unstrictly. The three of them ate fast bent silent.

The Father loved too many people was his problem not his only one either he knew. Skirting the bedlam shore of the lake he and Shannon Wells walked shoulder to shoulder like a little newlywed couple shy about bed linens and nakedness. They had things to talk about specifically with each other but didn't know how to talk about them yet. No guarantee they ever would.

Mostly the difficulty in speaking though came from his knowing she was more than a kid and he could not speak to her like one. How do you talk to one who knows just the same stuff as you except to be quiet with them and let the knowing do its work.

The Father and Shannon Wells came to rest in wooden Adirondack chairs facing the water. The men who often fished there rode the backs of the chairs low so now the two of them slipped back into the curves of the chairs until all they saw were the heads of the undeveloped cattails leaning around to converse with one another and the cloudless sky it was still early the sun was a little weakling beam the stars had yet to diminish fully but twinkled at half-brightness mumbling rumors of light.

He was thinking of the way she did it this time with Edna's pills it was an awfully quiet way to do it to go and be gone.

You'd think I was getting the hang of this thing she said. Of dying. Of course dying is gonna happen people get so scared they forget their cool unless they've got the misfortune of facing it more than once and see I've been practicing.

He sighed. I wish I knew what was happening here I try to pray about it.

I wish I could help you but all that I know what to do is die. She reached up to mark a small circle on her white throat with her thumbs. I'm not even really good at that. You're good enough to give us trouble. Not good enough to stick the landing. Ha we shouldn't joke about it don't you think do you feel bad joking about it.

It's very funny she admitted.

The Father pressed his lips together listened because he had no bone in him to laugh by and required a serious thing. Heard usual frightening noises of water slapping its body against the earth's bigger body. He translated easily into sentences in his head spoken in two voices.

He was a difficult case. This whole case was difficult. In the middle of life which was increasingly difficult. Shannon Wells kneeled her cheek on the heel of her hand. Glancing sideways at the Father she inspected his look an inverted one she didn't quite like for some reason on him. You can't solve death by taking blame she said. He stared at her. What makes you think I blame myself. Shannon said I don't know but it's my fault it started when I came here so don't you think if I moved away I would start dying. I don't think so.

They sat up and watched the soft windblown tide gnaw at the shore. The water slid between the reeds made them sing in hushed rough voices like paper windchimes.

After now the mornings will not be so silent.

Shannon Wells said you're right. A still warm silence lay breathing over the fields through their lonesome spot off the side of the country highway. Over the horizon geese squalled for an emptier place in the hills.

Not worth mentioning his sermon about what it meant to roll away a stone there were some mutterings that it was a little late for an Easter service wasn't it. One occasion several months ago he'd stumbled through benediction and asked god to dissolve hearts instead of absolve them which was kind of funny but later cried about it in the housekeeping closet he'd really meant the mistake felt wrong to correct himself once it'd already been said and so shakily.

Four years now since he'd returned to Palmyra from apparently seminary his parents dead never came back he'd been young even then but accustomed to holding sorrow on his shoulders. When he was seen outside the church in those early days he lurched and hobbled haggardly about like some blind wretch desperately hoping to bump into any structure he might guide himself by. Now seemed resigned to whatever he carried. Sometimes stopping by the road he contemplated the unlikely flourishing of beautiful things.

Shannon Wells was fourteen when she arrived by taxi almost a year later fourteen the first time she died and came back.

She'd stood coming out of an airport taxi with her knees apart her fists balled at her sides. He'd seen her big pale face full of holy retribution and pride and her little lame eyes which appeared to him so gray they contained all the world's uncertainties. Her yellow ratty hair. He imagined her parents holding her down to tame it with a horsehair brush her fighting and biting the hands that bound her wherever it was she was bound.

He loved her not in the way that husband and bride loved but in the way half a face loved a remaining half how a dewdrop loved the sun it formed under.

Sometimes stopping by the road he contemplated the unlikely flourishing of beautiful things.

In the golden waist-high corn it wasn't yet summer because nothing had reached its fullest capacity for growth. The Coroner though he'd lived in Ohio almost all his life had lived only in its cities and did not know firsthand how high corn grew. Maybe up to his ears. Maybe ten feet tall. Maybe tall like beanstalks growing with giants' houses at the tops of them buried in cloudheads for little boys to clamber up and down toward heaven on toward heaven and back toward heaven and down. Made him tired just thinking about it but someone was out there thinking about it all the time right. He thought of the Father. The Father's mouth. Mouth of the Father. The corn lashing under sedan slipstream as he slid around easy state route corners. That morning the earth behaving as if waking from a deep sleep. In the golden country covering everything with corn-light touching objects leaves curves of faces intimately in intimate knowing. Rolled down window gasping in stuck his hand out fishing it around in the wind.

Hey how are you. He called the Father when he made it home and left a message on the machine because the Father was busy preaching.

The Coroner came back on a Tuesday not for Shannon but for himself. It was two hours there and two hours back but also a weekday he could speed a little cut it short. When he arrived the Father was sitting already on the porch step legs crossed hands fit together over his forehead brown hairs stuck through the gaps. Wearing this white button up with slight cream stripes probably looted from his great grandfather's wardrobe from before turn of the century. Whittling out a tune with his toes on the grass. You look cool today the Coroner said I mean cool like temperature cold you know. I know. Are you cool. No the heat is oppressive today. They joined together the Coroner holding the Father's hand to help him stand up and after too until they parted ways at the hood of his car and tucked themselves inside it. Turned north for Gray but they weren't going to Gray. The Father said I think sometimes summer must be the earth's fever to get rid of all it doesn't need. He looked out the window. Back of his head to the Coroner chin propped in hand. The Coroner nodded. Then it's good we're still here right if you get that hot I have air conditioning see that knob there it makes you resistant to death. I don't think that's how it works. Sure it is in heaven it's god's knob but it's a knob just the same.

Exactly halfway between Palmyra and Gray the Coroner pulled onto the shoulder hitting a stacked cairn of gravel with the front left tire sprayed out scattered into the grass. Leaving the car he retrieved a pair of hedge trimming shears from the backseat. Passed them to the Father who tucked them into the waistband of his pants the wind took his shirt collar and lower unbuttoned triangles of fabric where the seams met blessed them with motion pulled them back turned them forward. The Coroner tipped his head saying wow. What is it. Nothing this wind is just the driest thickest wind I've ever been in like it's really actually heavy huh. I guess so it's been like this all week. Hey I can't stop looking at you. Oh. Oh. Oh yes well the Bible would say gouge your eye out. I'm not going to do that. That's fine I really wouldn't want you to which I guess makes me damneder.

The Coroner tipped his head the other way. They moved off the shoulder onto a path cut into the fledgling midsummer cookout corn kept down with sparse scales of gravel. You're a real funny man. I think you're mistaken I feel so tired lately I feel thinner. That's a good thing usually. No my soul feels thinner not my body and I can catch my breath fine you don't have to slow down.

Kept their heads down most of the walk there. The Father had longer legs but the Coroner had more energy so they kept pace if watchful of one another and they were. At the end of the path about two miles spindled out into a copse of farmland trees maintained to prevent good soil from wasting away like the dustbowl days just a few maples and oaks and walnuts and a dense untended mat of undergrowth. Skunk cabbage ivies thistle early unbloomed goldenrod cow parsnip. The path cut into these a little bit but mostly the Coroner and the Father stepped over them. Fragrant crushing with booted feet snap of green bodies breaking. He hadn't wanted to step on them just over. They'll grow back said the Coroner like wildfire. No like wildflowers. I told you you're a real funny man. I didn't mean it as funny. A little way into the copse a fence broken and only mid-calf high. They lifted their knees to cross it. Inside the skunk cabbage ivies thistles early unbloomed goldenrod cow parsnip almost obscuring several miniature headstones. Evidently old some of them set in marble and real rock. A few exacted from granite but still buried in wildflowers just the same. The Father knelt down pulled the shears from his trousers and gently hacked away at lower stems. Grabbing the tops of flowers like the hair of children pulling them exposing secret knots of secret play.

As the Father worked the Coroner lay on his back in a thicket of pale flat-headed cow parsnip bowing heads plucking them off between his fingernails setting them on his chest. When he breathed they shared his breath peering over the grass and sinking slowly down again. In a low mumble saying if summer is really a sickness as you said I think

I'd rather never be healthy again. All seasons need moderation and I'm glad for it. You would be there's not much else to excite you out here apart from when I'm around Edna told me the other day all you ever do during the week is mope through town looking for things and she doesn't know what you're looking for she wanted me to ask maybe she has it at her farmhouse in a cupboard somewhere probably too high for her to reach Shannon will have to give her a boost on her back. I'm not looking for anything I'm looking for the opposites of things. Seems nonsensical to me. The Coroner brushed the flowers from his ribs and rolled onto his stomach staring through tall scrub at the Father's bent head which the walnut trees crowned in branches and fresh tennis ball excellence. Behind him a clear sun painting the sky blue in steady capable wide hands. The Father looked very pretty slouching at his work like an illuminated portrait of the Virgin Mary in a catholic parish a face of round edges made of liquid light. The opposite of things is nothing at all. Yes just like the opposite of life is death but don't they complement one another. What's the exact verse on that. I am he that liveth and was dead and behold I am alive for evermore amen. Are you really happier when I'm around. Yes when you're not around I get to thinking that you can't possibly be happier when I'm around it's mostly all the things I can't give you. You could give me the opposites of things only you could do that. If I could find them. If you could find them.

On their way back from the old joint cemetery they came across Edna and Shannon walking the berm to Gray in over the ankle leather boots and matching paisley sundresses their hair pushed back in hats. Edna wearing old black beaver thing clearly the Old Father's clearly meant for funerals. Her surly hair tucked up in it so only feathery bits showed soft around the tops of her ears. Shannon wearing a baseball cap with her bun pulled through the hole. The Coroner coasted alongside them window already rolled down hanging his elbow out he asked do you need a ride into town. Edna said of course so they got in the backseat. Shannon Wells moved the shears from the floor into her lap. Nice dress said the Coroner and she shrugged. She don't prefer dresses she prefers shorts. Edna made me wear it. To impress that store boy. To impress that store boy exactly his name is Ian but I couldn't give a rat about no store boys no dresses I'll up and get naked right in the store before I wear this thing ever again. Shannon Agnes Wells you'd better not. To that she said nothing but played with the greened legs of the Father's shears between her fingers. You don't got to wear it ever again Edna conceded. Alright then.

Gray was 1500 citizens stronger than Palmyra meaning they had a population of exactly 1551 including the boy Ian Macgregor whose grandparents came over from Scotland in the 1900s and who did not like to be working in a shop off the state route selling essential items such as chicken feed milk bottles mason jars light bulbs toothbrushes tampons and everything. He would likely long remain in Gray out of filial obligation and for that reason the Father felt close to him pitied his condition his untempered sarcasm his coping mechanisms and his general teenage meanness. It's understandable he wanted to say I would've been the same as you if I was perhaps less inhibited or a different person entirely if I was allowed to be that. But would he really want to now that was a question he hadn't yet determined the answer to. The store was called Macgregor's. This was chosen by the first Macgregor to ensure that someone in the family always took it up it wouldn't make sense to customers any other way.

When the four of them walked through the front door a little bell went off hung up by an intricate string and pulley mechanism Ian had manufactured in his abundant spare time. Shannon Wells locked eyes with him right away didn't say a word. He smiled at her. You look like a right country skank Shannon. I look like your old ma I bet she's the skankiest skank if I ever seen one. Edna clapped the back of her head with an open palm hissed you better start behaving yourself miss be polite. He wasn't polite to me first. It don't matter you take it to task to be first polite yourself.

I would say sorry for calling your ma a skank said Shannon but I ain't really and Ian said okay I ain't sorry either and they grimaced shyly at one another. You know what I don't get is people not minding their own business. Will you be at school again in August or did you decide to get homeschooled after all. This is exactly what I mean. I know you reminded me of it if you come back you could join track with me or they might make a lacrosse team its real rough they might not let girls join but I think you could. What's that supposed to mean. I'm just saying. What are you just saying. Jesus Christ It was a complement I swear. I might come back to school if you let me borrow your daddy's golf cart sometime. No way what for Shannon really now what would I do that for.

Edna The Father the Coroner ducked behind the half-stocked shelves picking dry groceries together. A hand bumped into a hand. Whose hand was that sorry. On the way home this stiff and holy silence pervading the Coroner's sedan's interior also some off-brand cereal can of alfredo sauce pectin box of trash bags.

In the evening she was dancing dancing with no clothes on and then she leaned out the attic window fell three stories broke her jaw her spine her collar but was still alive. She bled a long time.

Mostly internal bleeding said the Coroner later. He explained how a rib invented its method to puncture her lung. Leaning hard on the Father's shoulder touching the sheer cream stripes of his shirt with delicate fingertips. Breathed in deep. Kissed his neck. Is that supposed to make me feel better the Father said on a little sigh. No I guess not I just thought you ought to know. Okay thank you for telling me. That's okay I'm sorry you're welcome. How long until she's healed up this time. Couple of days maybe a week unless she dies somehow then only twelve hours or so the injuries are pretty extensive. That ain't too long. No it isn't.

How long would it take to puncture the lung of someone you had no intentions of hurting to let the breath slide right out of him through some unnatural hole how tight would the Father have to hold the Coroner's middle or chest wherever he could find ribs to break. Of course he wouldn't break his ribs that's the thing about having no intentions of hurting but the thought crossed his mind anyway that every vulnerability brought with it the power of great breaking. The Coroner could break him. You could break me he said quietly you could break me very easily any time you really wanted to couldn't you you're strong enough. On his back now the Coroner on top of him paused tipped his head the heel of one hand steadied on the Father's forehead. It's more to do than strength. I know but you could. I won't. But you could.

Are you afraid of all men as you are of me. More and less afraid. You'd be no fun at a mall or museum that's for sure you'd better find the rapture before you find a business meeting. Yes. Are you alright. I don't know I'm a conflict of interests at my basest nature and I do wonder sometimes that the anxiety hasn't killed me yet it certainly hasn't killed me I'd have known if it had but I wish it would I wish it would kill us both for good. Hey I always tell you if you need a break to settle yourself just let me know you worry me much more than Shannon.

The Father looked up at the Coroner hurriedly and with sincerity and mourning in his eyes there was always some degree of it there he wore and it dragged him down like a specter or lurch of a man. I've made my decision about you even if I haven't made up my mind he said but you should go for now you work early. I guess I do. Are you mad at me. No I'm not it's okay I understand. No you don't really. Okay then I guess not.

He walked the Coroner to his car it was dark past midnight and he couldn't see any neighboring lights on in windows save for Edna's bedroom he knew she would be awake anyway waiting for Shannon to rise up the Coroner kissed the Father's cheek got into his car into the departing lane of the country highway his headlights cutting smart white shapes on the concrete diminishing as he drove away.

They'd met the second time Shannon Wells hanged herself only the second time she died she was less imaginative then less careful too everything to her seemed less necessary. Edna asked the city personally to send a different coroner maybe a young one claimed they had trouble with the last she neglected to mention the same person had died after fluke prognosis of week prior so they sent the newest and youngest they had who knew how to keep little secrets needing to be kept which was convenient for everyone. He'd recently left school and still remembered how to ask for things and when.

He showed up ahead of police force nervous about being late just a spit of dubious Peruvian heritage black hair big brown eyes and the city van. Edna asked where are the police he said I don't know not here yet by the looks of it I'd guess still driving here then. She said come in. He entered the blue farmhouse he didn't remove his shoes there were paper slipcovers on them. She pointed him in the direction of her landline still a rotary phone from her parents said you'd better call the police and tell them they don't got nothing to come for then I got to talk to you about something sir. The Coroner so surprised to be called sir did exactly as told the police didn't come and Edna sat him at her dining table told him all about Shannon Wells. The Father was there mediating or interpreting he didn't quite know. Edna sometimes struggled to find words and was under the assumption people went to college for that exact kind of thing. It wasn't like that she should know he'd left for so many years never talked to her or wrote to her once never talked to anybody from Palmyra and when he got back divorced her without saying why. He was improbably the worst communicator at the table but when she nudged him nodding trailing off on a long breath he can tell you what I mean he always picked up well what she means to say sir is simply this. And it seemed to satisfy her.

The Coroner assumed still married when he saw them sitting there together the Father wearing a ring he asked how long later the Father leading him up the attic stairs to Shannon's room where she lay. We're not anymore we're divorced. So the Coroner knew the Father was a complicated man.

Why do you still wear the ring he asked two months later leaning out his car window after a prolonged awkward goodbye he wasn't particularly certain the meaning of it yet he thought maybe the Father was a very lonely man not knowing how to make a friend. The Father said because I'm sorry I had to do it. Do what. Divorce Edna. If you're so sorry then why did you have to do it. Because I just ain't meant for people I suppose I'm meant to be lonely for a long time I don't know why but it seemed like something I should do and that I was capable of doing there aren't very many things I'm capable of besides I'd left her lonely for so long she deserved not to be tied to someone like me who caused her so much pain and that I really was sorry for so I had to leave her because I couldn't say I wouldn't do it again. Wow that's the most I've ever heard you say. Sorry. No don't be sorry I want to hear it we should talk again soon like this. I don't know about that. Why not.

The next few weeks they did talk again like that a little later dusk like a busy palette behind the Father's head the light in the attic on the Coroner asked again why not. The Father shook his head walked away a few feet returned let himself into the passenger seat. Can you drive for a while he said because I like you. You generally talk again to people you like. No you know how I mean please just drive I can't think properly here I need to get out farther than I can walk myself away. I'll take you to my place. You'd better not. So they drove past the cemetery past Gray to a small college town with a roundabout in the center The Coroner driving around it until they both grew dizzy and needed to park get out stretch their legs walk in the night by the closed shop windows together saying nothing at all.

At the car again the Father saying sorry. The Coroner looked up from his feet into the Father's eyes small watery blue-gray almost Shannon's not quite. What for. I'm sorry I can't talk to you anymore. Sure you can I like you too. No I really can't I have to be what I am I have to be for Palmyra. I won't tell. I know you won't and I want to save you from it. From not telling. From having not to tell

I know what it's like myself that and not being able to tell because it's something you can't say with any word at all so you don't want to do this

really.

So he came around more often. This was what he saw him like. In the house in the evening. Over light on his face soft purple and gray striations of pretty gold moving as snow and branches moved like

shadows from water from the lake on the ceiling sometimes in summer
lying on the floor in his bedroom the light would move like snake scales
sliding with subtle noises of no aquatic life. In the heat and coolness of
that distant illumination he always thought afterward of the Coroner
offering the next time he was in Palmyra after that night. Anything at
all really he said can I do anything at all for you. That's a lot to ask but
I'll try and think of something surely there are things needing done
around here I guess you can start with feeding the hens. I've never seen
a hen in my life. The Father had nothing to say so he stared. Of all
shocking concepts.

He went out with him to the henhouse showed him where feed was
kept in a silver waste bin weighed down with a rock showed him how
to remove the rock and toss the feed at which point it would've been
more expedient to do it himself but he did like the way the Coroner
watched him swing his arm out for the hens. I get it now he said. There's
not much to get it's pretty simple like I said as long as you ain't scared
of chickens. I ain't scared of chickens said the Coroner putting on the
Father's voice and the Father stared at him again. What is it. Nothing
I think. You're giving me a specific look. What look is it I'm sorry. No
I don't mind it I like it actually it's a look like. Like what. Like I don't
know I'm just getting to know you. Okay well tell me when you figure it
out. It's important for you to know things about yourself. Yes it is.

It was a look like the Coroner held some fact about the Father that
he hadn't known before or else had not been aware of wandering to find
so what if there was something soft and comfortable about it. He wanted
to sleep in whatever feeling his look responded to he wanted to have the
Coroner know strange upward feeling maybe it was a look of love.

In the morning sun was simple fallen on Palmyra even rising up from
it to return from where it'd come. The Father saw through his kitchen
window. On the lake like a bed of scales. It really was beautiful and
terrifying he thought of mysterium tremendum a word for when people
saw god. Indescribable beauty terror love bound up in one no other
word or feeling like it.

On the lakeshore when he was a kid his mother crouched down chasing him with her gardening glove worm in her hand I'm going to get you I'm going to get you I'm going to get you laughing her smile like spread butter on her own child-face. Tackled to the earth the worm end slipping against his cheek oh I got you didn't I didn't I tell you I would that's what you get for running.

The Old Father standing at the back door arms folded but also smiling were things simpler then he didn't know he wished he could know or make them less complicated in retrospect but things in retrospect were always more complicated than they seemed when they happened. Two summers ago. It'd been him hadn't it. Who leaned over pressed the back of his hand to the Coroner's collarbone asked very quietly I'd like to try something if that's alright. The Coroner keeping space between them tending it a precaution learning a slow pace. Are you sure he asked and the Father thumbed over the corner of his right eye somehow even quieter echoing back are you sure.

Really the Coroner said he said it without laughing so then the Father kissed him. He said after that it was good it was very good.

He did his dishes slow watching for the light changing as morning went on.

Shannon collected bugs. Keeping them for up to a week sometimes in the tank in her bedroom. The mesh lid barely registered like a feather the air blew through when she tested and weighed it in her hands. Hence the rock from Edna's garden perched always on the corner. Scared the bugs would get out and crawl into her ears which is what her ma told her when she was very young and her ma very young too almost too young to have a daughter and what Edna told her when she caught her bringing distasteful bugs in the farmhouse. Distasteful bugs including but not limited to spiders bees wasps water boatmen beetles larger than two thumbnails across. Unfortunate because these happened to be the best bugs for observation. When she finished observing she took photographs on her Polaroid which the strap had rotted off of she'd tied it up with an old monogrammed guitar strap belonging to nobody. Being then done with the bugs she turned the poor harassed things out in Edna's back garden but often they'd already forgotten what it was to move freely and acted still as if four invisible walls blocked them into the tomato patch not eating anything but spinning their heads in circles like they were looking to.

When she recovered from her fall the Father brought her a common grub in a blue plastic pail coming up to her attic room stooping to fit under the angled ceiling beams he sat in a wooden chair broken so it barely supported his weight he placed the bucket between his knees. How are you feeling he asked. She narrowed her eyes. Sore real sore. That's hardly surprising. Shows you not to ask questions you already know the answers to oh and you put that right in the tank. Alright I will.

She'd captured the common grub's portrait already tucked in the back pocket of a binder for the explicit purpose of insect portraits kept in the primest spot on her bookcase. Kept that portrait behind everything else to avoid looking at it. She didn't envy or enjoy the lives of larvae. Such creatures living without eyes in the dirt and mud of the planet eating pure mineral and eaten in turn by anything with a mouth big enough to swallow them and some things without mouths big enough they made no sound lived in false bodies which softly split open without protest as soon as the true inner body fulfilled its final hardness.

The Father removed the rock from the top of the tank gently peeled back the mesh angled the bucket in sideways the grub still inside and the bucket also now in the tank. Thanks said Shannon. You're welcome I thought it might give you something to look at. You could've caught a dragonfly or something that moves. I wasn't fast enough I did try. Now he was apologetic again. She blinked at him. You did try that's alright.

He didn't return to his broken seat elected instead to stand with his hands clasped a tiny tent or temple a partial viewing window to his belt buckle. Head half-bowed she wondered why didn't he sit down on her level. So why again he said. I don't know I was just dancing and lost track of myself you know how it is. I hardly ever lose track of my body I'm very aware of it. No you ain't. I am. You've told me otherwise

before. No I told you I don't feel connected sometimes to it there's this
dream I have. What's the dream of. I don't know I'm afraid to say.

They kept silence a while then the Father left down to his yard
throwing feed out to chickens under the yellow noon sun. Thinking
of blessings hermeneutical spirals atomic structure and separation.
Shannon thinking in the attic of the blue farmhouse of homes and
when on earth would she feel like getting up getting that big plastic
bucket out of her tank out of the way.

To describe the Coroner's apartment in one word was economy. The
Father in many ways fit just the same but the Coroner's spacious
economic upward organization his lack of place but being settled all the
same so comfortably into it frightened him reminded him of seminary.
So when the Father needed to speak without being in Palmyra they
went either to the cemetery or drove a little parked and sat in the car
someplace today was a day for the latter they parked on the berm
between two corn fields leaned the seats back a few inches rolled each
of four windows down let the emptiness roll through over their chests
like it was stepping on them making them breathe. Looking at one
another over the center console but not touching.

The Coroner said how's she feeling. Better now said the Father.
How are you feeling. Pressed upon. What's that supposed to mean you
have to elaborate. I don't want Shannon to die. I know but who does
want that. Shannon wants to die and if I wanted what she wanted if
I wanted what was best for her wouldn't I want that too and what if I
figured out why this was happening would knowing the truth give me
the power to make it untrue if I knew the truth would I lose Shannon
would I lose my friend. Do you want to know the truth. Yes I do. Why.
I feel like I'm missing something massive I need to be a part of me.
The truth. Yes the truth needs to be a part of me and anyway is it even
right for this to happen. For people to live again. Yes I don't know the
ethical implications of such a place as Palmyra and the circumstances
here. The Coroner laughed and said if Shannon is a natural occurrence
as she seems to be then it should be alright super-ethical nature is far

more concerned with ethics than we are. Now you have to explain what you mean by that. I mean nature is the final ethic isn't that Biblical. I suppose you're right if I understand you proper. I think you do you're a smart man.

The Father wide and fearful in the passenger seat breathing slow his lungs barely visible beneath the wind his shirt his skin his ribs he knew these vague notions of wanting to say more. He blinked slow. He hoped the Coroner would understand him would understand this big vastness a big empty room in his chest inside him. Oh god oh god oh god he thought what do I want to love you putting his fingers out the gap between pointer and middle on the center console the Coroner laying his fingers over top not holding but covering his fingertips warm with heartbeats. I'm sorry the Father whispered but it did not mean what he needed it to.

If you want to figure this out I'll help you. Okay we should at least try it's only right that we make an effort of things. I think you're right about that too said the Coroner smiling at himself because the Father did not smile back. Quiet for several hours just lying there. Once another car passed by.

Goofy rubber limbed rosy limbed children running around each other at the edge of the lake at sunset. End of the day the shade of imminent destruction orange red liquid air thick and dusky. Singing I would lock you in my arms if you would let me. If you walked into my arms I would lock you in. Loudly a smaller voice singing darling clementine getting the words wrong. All of a sudden Shannon coming down from her room she sat in the grass in the Father's backyard then very slowly stood up. The children kept running pretending to be even more afraid.

Here is what god used to look like was what the dream seemed to try to tell him but he didn't understand what it was saying through the pictures it put him in and it never said anything about what god looked like now.

He woke sweaty in the middle of the night. Sat up so shocked fast in bed the sheets fell into his lap and then he was suddenly cold and sweaty which was worse. The blinds open. Alone in the house except for the dream present with him still reclining in his bed undisturbed by his quickness the quickness of his heart.

In the dream leaving his soul's body in bed and exploring the earth without it. And the earth was loved. In this dream he felt his essence pull into three distinct pieces and he went with the piece that was unconditionally him above great waters. And the waters were loved. This dream also took place before all creation. And creation was loved most of all and who was that hovering within it like the misty halo sparkling round the playtime sprinkler. He knew this dream had been before anything else had been and what he saw beyond overbig images what he heard in lightest whispers travelling clear over the switchbacks of waves he couldn't remember but someone had loved him then when he hadn't wanted them to.

He got up dressing in the dark in whatever sat on his dresser from last evening went out stood in his lawn and the grass reached higher than his ankles without looking back at his house he started down the road north sticking to the grassy berm traveling at a lopsided jog.

Two miles out breaking into a loping sprint for five minutes in five minutes managing to sweat through his clothes the sweat clinging to his forehead sticking to his hair in streaks. Wiped them away with his wet forearm and slowed to a walk. He favored one foot. The other turning out awkwardly from his knee. As he walked he thought about home until his thoughts filled with vacuums of memory and blackness but one memory jumped out to him through this dim smoke of the Old Father crouching with him in a stand in the woods in southern Ohio close to the West Virginia border each of them with a shotgun stock pressed to their dominant shoulder and on one knee they peered out onto a flat grassy circle in the woods where wild turkeys grazed their soft necks bent in the white sunlight thrumming with heartbeats and muted squabble. The Old Father said you have it now shoot and the Father said no. Somewhere a brook rolled over woody knots and the water's soft speaking dissipated broadly over the forest. Then what Benjamin Jonah Lythgoe do you reckon you're going to eat the Old Father said. The Father said I guess nothing. He wondered always after what and how much of it needed eating to stay alive. Alive being a big and general term its own question nobody knew the answer to his original response still seemed in some ways proper to him. Consuming he guessed nothing. In the midst of his remembering this he followed a little shadow of his own invention or of coal black rage fueling him forward so that each step unstiffened he was like a ribbon of serpents propelled down the road by a befanged battle of wills spiting and biting one another.

He eased off the road near a swatch of wheatgrass painted silver and smoothed of flaws in the nighttime. Insects sang drunken songs in the stalks and the stalks sang their own song of being brushed together. He walked a path through the field and eventually came to the little graveyard plot by the walnut trees. He entered through the gate standing open wailing in the warm wind.

Now that he'd arrived he'd lost the notion of what he came for. The energy behind his anger had vacated several miles back on the road leaving in its place a jagged hole filled partway with a small smooth stone of frustration. He gripped the tops of his parents' headstones one in each hand intent on drawing them together or uprooting them from the ground as molars uprooted from gums leaking coagulated strings of blood behind but his body refused to corroborate these desires so he stood arms and sides stitched bracing himself upright against the headstones.

Edna stepped from behind a tree. The Father sat down. Nothing could surprise him here if he saw several ghosts dance out hand in hand and invite him into their waltz he would say I'm not astonished and think about saying yes.

Edna said showing her palms I saw you and I hid I don't know why you looking like you did running down here would get anyone frightened I hardly recognized you until you were standing this close. She held her fingers apart displaying the closeness to be less than an inch in length.

The Father felt disgusted at having been found here at this hour and sorrow that he'd been found by her and shame at everything else.

What are you doing here he asked. Just like you weeping. That's not like me.

He guided himself slowly on hands and knees into damp grass in the center of the cemetery and she joined him leaning against his shoulder with one shoulder of hers. You know I was born two things and only one of them was a Christian child of god I wish people weren't born anything at all you think we can choose to do certain things well we can't he said but he saw that this sort of speech upset her and changed his tone saying god giveth and god taketh away sometimes when he taketh it's actually he's just giving us what we never thought not to want. She said why's things got to be the way they are with you and me and with Shannon. I don't know why with Shannon I guess with me it's because I deserve hardship as much as any person. But not more than that. But I got what I got Ed.

She thought about what he said. You're awful brave. I don't know what you mean I'm not brave because I'm not courageous I'm just a person and as scared of anything as you are. I know you're scared of everything. Not everything. Of dying. Yes I suppose one day it might be all of us. It's not enough you know it's not enough. He looked away.

He did know it wasn't enough. He didn't know what would be enough but he didn't possess it as surprised as he was that he possessed the strength to get to the cemetery in the first place. While he was there the air was full of rushing as speechless wind sucked at the switchgrass and a thin halo encased half the moon but it was a trickery heat played on those awake so late he didn't feel god here or within twenty miles of here he'd never felt god in his life but once though occasionally occupationally speaking he was obliged to.

The Father stood picked Edna up by her elbows helping her out of the cemetery. Walking together bumping bodies back through the grass and at the road they walked on opposite sides and the return journey felt twice as long for each of them as the journey there.

———

Guilty oh no. Please don't dissolve on him. I'm sorry so sorry at the door and she forgave him again but what for anymore there was so much be forgiven for. His body absolutely heavy with it again and again sinking to the bottom of the lake.

One night early last summer. The Coroner having come such a long way for Shannon sky a heavy shade of shadow fighting back any reference of time.

Do you want to go for a drive or something the Coroner asked the Father on his way out because he was lingering again though they'd discussed so many times why he shouldn't and couldn't when they spoke every night on the phone. I think so but the Father said. But what. I don't really got any place in mind. Easy then we'll just drive get on in. You sure. Yes sir.

Drove to a gas station twenty minutes out for the Coroner to buy fuel for the ride home later. While he paid inside the Father leaning against the fuel tank watched a balloon's ribbon twitch stuck in the overhead lighting above pumps he wondered how long. Air clinging and hot like fur. When the Coroner returned it started immediately to rain. Filled up the tank watched for a while under the overhang as the deluge pulled mud into the street. The Coroner sighed alright we better be getting back this is a mess say a quick prayer for us will you. Oh god rectify these tires and make straight our path and thank you for this reminder that the angels enjoy their evenings off just like the rest of us and are indeed still in your presence bowling he said raising his hands to the rain and the Coroner laughed. My mom used to tell me that too he said that whenever there's thunder the angels got a strike. It's all I can think about sometimes. The Coroner laughed again.

On the county road could barely see five feet ahead. Some minivan in the distance kept its hazards flickering staying lines of otherwise guideless automobiles. The Coroner drove careful but he did drive the speed limit wherever he was able he asked the Father ever learn how to pull out of a hydroplane. Never got my license. I'll take you out when the weather's better. A little while later coming upon a clog in traffic a semi had swiped some sedan into the irrigation ditch in the police lights could barely see the air bags engaged filling the interior up cops conducting cars telling them to keep moving. The Coroner slowed. Makes you wonder what happened there he said. Some disaster. Should we stop. Us. I suppose you have a point a coroner and some small-town preacher we may as well mark them for death. You have medical experience at least. Yes but in my limited experience with medicine I have found that people in pain mostly prefer religion. Especially on county roads I think. Oh yes especially.

Acorn drop knock of big dark rain kept coming. Public radio announced three inches a minute. The Father called ahead on the Coroner's cellphone had Edna switch on her porch light so they could find it to park by. This worked somehow but walking across to the Father's house drenched them both filled the tight spaces in the marrow of bones with rainwater cold eclectic dense. You can't drive home tonight said the Father standing in the foyer trying to remove his shoes and socks several pounds heavier. I don't have anything to wear here. You can borrow something of mine. I don't know. No good man would send you out there tonight it might take you hours to get home in this weather and what if you hydroplane. Then I'd steer into the skid. Huh. Okay where's your dryer.

Later in bed together for the first time laying a foot apart the way two girls sharing a bed at a slumber party do until someone closed the gap the Father didn't remember who. Invisibly nudged together. The Coroner's skull hard under his chin. Very warm and the sound of rain and thunder. You're funny said the Coroner. Why now. Tempting me this way having it rain so I would be here. Tempt is a funny word you know they always said in seminary the devil makes the best preacher. Why's that. He wields knowledge of the good book where the rest of us simply store it away and sometimes even pretend we don't know it so we can have the things we want. I didn't mean to make you upset sorry. It's okay. Anyway tempting wasn't necessary. Unfortunately I know that too.

The Coroner's hand moving a circle on his arm. Do the things you want make you happy. They do make me very happy or else I wouldn't want them. What's the matter. I want to stay here. We are. I mean I want this and he took the hand the Coroner had placed on him. The Coroner thinking about making a joke but deciding not to. Okay he said instead you can have it whatever you want from me I'm giving to you. That's not fair.

The question on his mind was when would he take and take too much and could you leave something so desolate it ceased existing in its original form. In bed wrapped around the Coroner he thought of Edna turning on her porch light for him consoling himself thinking also she might've done the same for anyone. An indiscernible action in the long dark no matter the intention vanishing underneath guiding someone home. Okay it said. You can have it.

Surprise party at the end of the month of June for Shannon's eighteenth birthday. Edna told him the next day over breakfast while Shannon still slept hadn't come down yet or even made a stirring in the attic which creaked so they could tell when she'd be coming down maybe in another hour. Why a surprise do you think she'll actually like that sort of thing said the Father. Edna shrugged. I figure she needs the surprise whether or not she wants it. Is that how it works now. She gave him a sharp look pointed her frying pan at him. Don't you she said hard and nothing else just let it hang there and complete itself as he imagined.

She started on crepes. Made crepes whenever she expected the Coroner over thought it made her seem more dignified like she knew anything about city culture other than what sometimes came on radio or television shows but she didn't have a television just watched black and white film programming at the elderly neighbor's house on Thursdays and assumed all cities were sort of French sophisticated. The Coroner didn't know he just liked crepes the Father felt not mighty enough to ever disrupt her beliefs.

Okay he always said crepes. There were fresh strawberries from her garden sitting on a stained pink wet paper towel.

The Coroner walked in took off his boots at the door stood in the kitchen in a pair of discolored crew socks his work slacks a shirt tucked in which he quickly untucked revealing a kidney-shaped dark brown stain near the bottom hem. You couldn't have done your laundry Edna accused. He shrugged apologetically said couldn't have packed a spare shirt either. You're lucky I keep inviting you over here with manners like that. Thank you Edna said the Father. Come on now said Edna.

I've been re-reading Mitford lately said the Coroner and Edna said she'd been re-reading Albom. Oh which one. Tuesdays with Morrie and I just finished the Five People you Meet in Heaven. Those are pretty good.

When breakfast finished and the back garden needed pruning in the strawberry and blueberry patches and the grapevines and the wild raspberries which grew somehow inexplicably and weren't put down and rarely tamed the Father went out with the Coroner the two on their hands and knees in greenness the Father asking what about Mitford. She wrote a book I'm reading called the American Way of Death. What sort of things does she say that you're thinking about them. She says funeral men tend to invent the law as they go along and the Coroner laughed mostly I think she's a crackpot so what are you reading. Rilke. You've been reading poetry. No I've been reading his prose. That explains why you're so dramatic then just joking you know what sort of things does he say are you thinking about them deeply I'm sure. He says god is distant and the man who looks for him is lonely and needs to be forgiven. Do you think that's true. I haven't been entirely forgiven so I don't really know yet.

Saturdays in Palmyra concerned themselves mostly with righteousness meaning the righteous use of time. Sunday was Sabbath meant for righteous dutiful rest and a sermon before it. Most of Saturday then the Father spent in his study preparing notes accumulated on corners of paper napkin newspaper and steno pads throughout weekdays condensing them into notebooks into a single speakable sermon having to pull sometimes from previous weeks contemplations categorized with tabs according to relative subject matter on his top bookshelf his study always scattered afterward and needing organized which he secretly did on Sundays. Edna on Saturdays walking to Gray where she worked at the post office approaching her twentieth year of employment. In her early years just out of school she remembered receiving shy letters from the Father explaining troubles and turmoiled thoughts spiritual quandaries his love of her human heart. Which later dissipated when he left all of a sudden for university then seminary. He hadn't even told her he was going his mother told her several days later coming out the front door seeing her standing in the lawn oh sweetie he had to leave and they both wept embracing one another at life's great mysteries and losses.

It was on Saturdays the Father's mother used to come to the blue farmhouse though the Father couldn't have known this. Back in the long twilights of his absence. Edna worked through the daylight walked home to dinner with his mother always roasted potatoes and chicken her favorite until she wasn't able to chew anymore. They'd look across at the Old Father's bedroom light shaded behind the bedroom curtains and once Edna let his mother braid her hair on the couch in the library under her grandmother's pearly lampshade and today at the post office behind the picture window full of glare and country sunlight she remembered what his mother's arthritic fingers felt like sifting through her hair. Was this the last another grown person touched her. Timid clicking of knuckles at the follicles circling her ear. When Ian came in to send rebate coupons for his dad in curling envelopes salvaged from probably the bottom of the drawers of time Edna made a point to glance his palm with her fingertips taking his pocket change for a spare stamp but he left shaking out the offended hand and anyway it wasn't right. This wasn't what she wanted she thought to herself opening and shutting the spare stamp drawer beneath the perfect steel scale refracting fingernails of noontime sunlight that she ought to start giving to charity or something. What would god do. Probably sleep in a garden or kiss a disciple or overturn tables getting his anger all over the place. Now there was a comfort. But that wasn't it either. Now Edna thought what was worth all this time.

Shannon on Saturdays found things to do. Every other week Robbie Lou who fished on the lake paid her twenty dollars and a special quarter from his collection to mow grass not even in his own yard most times but she almost had all fifty of his special quarters now and was growing bored. So this Saturday she stripped down to her underclothes in the Father's backyard took a running leap into the lake. The Coroner came out the backdoor yelling what the hell do you think you're doing but she hadn't heard underwater when she reemerged headfirst soaked her tied hair heavy and limp he repeated what the hell do you think you're doing. Going for a swim mister. Do you frequently do this getting naked in other people's lawns. No but I figured I'd start the habit of it today want in. I don't want people getting the wrong idea. What's that supposed to mean. You're like half my age and naked. I'm not naked.

She crawled from the water dripping rose from a crouch to her knees to the balls of her feet dripping still the thoroughness of her soak making transparencies of her underclothes. Do you want a towel the Coroner asked she didn't answer but untied her hair got to ringing it out in the grass putting the tie back in but not as good this time a little crooked to the left. She trained a stare at him those thimble gray eyes all thinness and light. He felt no discomfort only amazement that one girl barely a woman scientifically interpersonally could cause so much yet so little to happen.

You want to see a place she asked. What kind of place. Just a place I know because I found it. Alright let's go do you want some clothes first. No. A towel. I really don't you can stop asking now.

She brought him across the street behind the blue farmhouse without knowing why she brought him. I'm showing you this because I'm bored she said but that wasn't really true she wanted the Coroner to see it. She brought him behind the garden of the farmhouse he'd helped prune brought him behind a wild hedge to a military organization of mistrusted cornrows and a yellow combine making tracks of dust. She went into the cornrows the Coroner hesitating behind her then going in too loud. Deep heavy footsteps. Pressure of corn leaves blading his forearms neck hands as he pushed them back. He kept up with her barely she was nearly the same color as the corn and easy to lose but he found her by rustlings if he listened close.

How far he asked. She called to him without looking back however far it is until we get to where we're going. That's really helpful. Hey I'll leave you behind so shut up. It wasn't much longer she broke through the corn then him she jogged across a thin division of grass he followed through the grass over a trunk fallen upon a thin perennial stream glutted with crawdads minnows tadpole children into sparse deciduous woods green and white light falling through growing little undergrowth patches in its weakness. Sounds of sparrows finches and somewhere a raccoon scrabbling for corn kernels in a tower he'd built from stolen husks. A little farther in this wood and they came to a house two stories tall with three front windows busted in glassless the doorframe empty and the roof coming down. Shannon entered in. The Coroner entered in. Who used to live here he asked. I don't know nobody probably or somebody real old from a long time ago. How long ago do you think. Maybe a hundred years ago like way before we were born. It can't be that old. I think it could. What makes you think that. The way it smells. Well okay then. Ian told me. Ah that makes more sense.

To discuss this house between the two of them who had no relation to it was to truly inhabit it the way time had to retract the undone spool of years to the house's first emptiness at the incumbency of its existence to first foundations and feet bearing its load into the loam. Like the way the Coroner had once sprawled on his stomach on his bedroom floor with his boyhood friends and maybe the Father used to do performing otherwise impossible surgery on cassette tapes with the backs of pencils pink and leaking pigment into the film so the memory surfaced always through a milky wash and eventually failed to surface at all. Altered to simplicity time had the mind of a missing child.

Shannon tried to reiterate as Ian had explained to her. Back then two or three generations ago Palmyra encompassed twice its current land mass and triple its current population and then I-70 was built and the war came and their little country highway was forty minutes out of the way. As Palmyra contracted in defense of its more vital shores houses on the boundaries wood paneled and original with frontier basements like this one were liquidated left abandoned the wood panels occasionally thrifted by residents in need of patching or rafters. Or as Shannon told the Coroner people used to live clear over here in the old times but don't no more because the road or something stupid like that. Does this house belong to anyone in town nowadays. Beats me nobody's told me or Ian or anyone else off for fooling around with it.

Smell of wet wood and soft things growing softer with age and even softer more you looked at them. Touch the wallpaper with your hand it gave a little. You could make it breathe. The Coroner walked lightly. It was a little house not much room and so so quiet.

So what do you do here he asked. She said I do this. Okay he said he thought that was only right.

This was the house god lived in. It loved to be empty and loved to be full mostly it loved just to be. I love to be it said I love to be and you with me and when you leave I know where you go to but I can't follow you there not this time no during this time I cannot follow you there.

Hello the Coroner teased his voice out long a purposeful echo in an already echoing room. Shannon called back hello hello. They ran around the house shouting at each other chasing the sound of disembodied voices around corners up down the stairs the Coroner's bouncing laugh a captured string. Is anybody home still laughing. This is a stick-up got any cash got any jewelry. Yeah this is a robbery. Is anyone home. I am. Who the hell are you. I'm me. Where where where. Hello.

Chasing each other out the house woods grass division cornfield caddy-corner farmhouse yard state route the Father's backyard and the Coroner disrobed before jumping in the lake.

He came in soaked found a towel in the Father's kitchen put it on his head to keep drops on himself. Leaving leaky footmarks on tile. In the Father's study lying on his back on the floor keeping clear of fanned out notes. The Father took a minute to look up. You're not wearing any clothes he said. No I'm not. You're wet. Yes I am. You went swimming. Yes I did.

Shannon remained crouching silent at the shore behind the Father's henhouse with the muted gibberish swallowing of the sleeping hens scratching their litter because and she knew this for sure hens only dreamed of being awake. Yards away Robbie Lou worked at his fishing shed door with a doorstop and rebar mechanism he jerry-rigged for undoing the lock. There was his bait and tackle Tupperware emerging in his hands from a high shelf and also his long dry fly rod. Naked but for his waders and underwear and a cord around his neck. He met Shannon's stare in the dark like a flashlight seeking out a crocodile's tapetum the crystal sclera of the inner eye. They were quiet. One knifeblade of light from the Father's window pried open the dark on the damp grass spread between them gentle clapping skin soft like friction and mumbling of genesis ex nihilo. God brought forth either love or disagreement. Rob spat into the water the loud tick of bursting surface tension causing Shannon to rise from hiding. Aw shoot he said I knew I saw you was there up to no good girl now come on out of that chicken shit and help start me a fire. I don't know how to start no fires. Nonsense all young people know how to rub two sticks together been the same since Bible times.

He showed her how with a den of kindling from deep inside his waders and sticks she gathered from farther up the yards. Chicken shit burns good if you wanna grab some of that Rob said. She spat like he did I ain't grabbing no chicken shit go grab some yourself. Instead he gave her his necklace a dangling ruin of flint and steel passed down from a camping store. Shannon didn't know how to use it but she knew how to try.

Did I tell you how long I been here asked Rob just making conversation tying his fly fumbling his small knock-kneed fingers. Shannon shook her head she didn't care much for old people tales. You gonna tell me the one about swapping your house for a mole. No little lady I ain't as old as that tale but I can tell you I knew the Father when he was just about as skinny and small as you and you remind me of how he was then. Bull hockey. She bent over their nest of tinder scraping his flint and steel ineffectively together in the dark throwing up yellow sparks swimming into thin air shaped like tiny fish but he had her attention. He said I done fished that son of a gun right up from this here lake one night and took him home and made him build his own fire just like you now. He wasn't in the lake you're lying. He sure was on my mammy's life. Your mammy's dead and gone you old fool. Sure is but so have you been little lady. Well tell me what was he doing in the lake then. The itch itch itch of her furious hands mortaring sparks from Rob's flint and steel necklace. He told her to ask the Father why he was in the lake and to stop chopping at that flint as if she was out chopping

firewood on the last night before winter. It's one long drag continuous
he instructed though she pretended not to pay Rob mind angry at him
for not finishing his story about fishing the Father from the lake.

Soon they had a night-fishing fire. Robbie's bare summer old man back
illuminated among the ungrown cattails freckles and liver spots. Bent like
a hunchback he was very patient there didn't seem to notice her anymore
crouched by the fire putting her hands out for more heat. Mosquitos pretty
bad tonight eating her alive she'd be itching for so many weeks applying
deodorant toothpaste mud to puckered red spots and scabs.

In darkness the slapping lake. Dark water like silk unbolted.
Wondered how deep it was. What if there was no bottom but then
again. She scratched the tender bridges of skin between her ribs. There
was nothing very interesting to her of the magnificent everlasting as
the Father would say in endlessness tonight of all places in his own
backyard. She thought he would be the one to know.

As for the Father it was good on Fridays Saturdays and Sundays when
the Coroner slept in his bed and had no other work to do but keep
him feeling whole and home like nothing ever happened to him like
nothing ever would steal out from behind him or his insides get ye
behind me damned past occurrences he was so satisfied he could almost
forget where he was and where he was not other times kept so silent
to himself and drowning in awkward lonely sadness like he didn't even
know death elsewhere could be. Sustainable he spoke clearly in sleep
sustainable. The Coroner shook him to wake him. Were you dreaming.
The Father sighed placed his head down again I don't know. You were
saying a word. Was I what was the word this time. Sustainable. I know
it. What were you dreaming of. I don't know. The Coroner shook his
head said no talk to me. But the Father only had one word tonight and
it was a prayer. Sustainable he whispered sustainable.

There was a wasp's nest in a certain tree in Meredith Stow's yard who
was a neighbor on the Father's side of the road and Shannon went to

it on Sunday morning with Ian knocked it down with a big branch
and they ran. Ah shit we forgot a jar said Ian when they'd come back
to Edna's front step out of breath crouching on their shins. Shannon
slapped her bare knees. Well she said darn. A little too late now anyway.
Right. My da's going to be real mad at us for missing church. You bet
he is he's going to beat your ass. He won't I'm a man now. Yeah right.
Really he calls me that I got puberty and everything. Gross. It happens
to everyone you know. Not me.

Ian scratched his elbow said you serious Shannon with deep
concern too deep for him. Yeah I am my doctor says I can't even have
kids ever not that I'd want any. By doctor she meant the Coroner he'd
told her last year after she'd recovered from a vehicular collision having
hurtled out in front of an Amish horse and buggy the horse's hooves
plummeting through her abdomen crashing through the doors of
certain nonvital organs.

Can you still like boys. No I don't like boys. Not even me. You're a
man aren't you. Oh right. Anyway the answer's still no I hate your guts.
Yeah I hate you too more than anything and he bumped shoulders with
her but she was sturdy and didn't topple. Do you want to go to church
now. We should.

Shannon took Ian to sit in the back pew next to the Coroner who
made room. Edna sitting in the front row heard them come in glanced
over her shoulder and gave Shannon a look that told her she'd hear
stern words later about personal choices.

The Coroner had back pew because when first he started coming
citizens of Palmyra and Gray assumed he wasn't an American citizen
and anyway he figured he should leave front pews for those not in
bed with the preacher. Shannon didn't know this thought he was
uncomfortable with god generally as she sometimes was at least their
idea of him. Ian didn't know the Coroner and broke off to find his da.

The Father fumbled through a sermon again but still a decent
enough sermon about Judas the garden god forgiveness. Tried to
convince himself. Adam and Eve in Eden ate from the only evil seed
ran and hid were naked there in a bush their foreheads pressed together
trembling weeping probably and god only wanting to talk to them. He

took his animals sat down in an open grove peeling the skins off what a bloody mess he'd made a sheep inside-out he stitched the skins together and presented them as a gift please take this it's for you I didn't want you to know shame please this hurts.

The Coroner drove Edna to a town beyond Gray to some bakery to order Shannon's birthday cake special. Shannon and the Father after church occupied his study placing dated papers in particular stacks.

We haven't talked in a while just the two of us. You've been busy. You can talk to me any time you don't have to wait for me not to seem busy.

Shannon said I've had other people to talk to. The Father laughed I heard already about the wasp's nest. Who saw. Robbie Lou. I should've known it. When I was a boy Ed and Will and I used to go around with a plastic bucket of rocks and throw them at wasp nests until they fell off the roofs and when all the wasps went away we collected the nests in a shoebox and floated them out on the lake like a little Viking boat. Couldn't you have just floated the shoebox. Yeah but we thought the nests made it lighter.

Holding up a torn notebook page she looked over the top at the Father looking at the floor. What would you do if you could do anything she asked. The Father horrified said what do you mean anything. Anything you wanted without nothing bad happening after. Like consequences you mean without consequences. Yeah sure consequences. I don't know. Why. I don't know what I want.

She put his page down. I do she said I guess that makes us very different then. She never thought about it before but she could pick a wasp's nest like an apple if she wanted to.

Edna's drive with the Coroner silent like a long stairwell. She never did know what to say to the man. A few times after his first visit with Shannon he came knocking on her door asking for permission to park in her yard sleep in his car there. She'd told him ain't no way you're doing that and brought him inside insisted him to her couch. She

thought it was strange someone would want to sleep in clothes they
intended to take on them to church the next day and never heard of
anybody sleeping in a car before when there were better places to go
it was good then that now the Father had him at church so often. In
the car he asked about how was her reading going. Admittedly she'd
finished all her unread books. On the way back he brought her easily to
Gray's library for more. So he at least knew something of kindness.

Are you okay he asked suddenly and just as suddenly was embarrassed
by it. A question he hadn't meant to ask. I mean you're quiet he adjusted
his seatbelt. I'm just fine don't you worry about it young man. She
wondered why she called him that still. Thought about several years
ago dialing a phone number and hearing a voice. Not just any voice the
impermeable unending river of a voice of the one she loved. Edna it said
dear sweet god are you okay. After all that time are you okay.

At home later in the night the front door unlocked and open she
turned on every light downstairs. Always expecting someone to return.
Come in pat down their shoes on the mat hang up their jacket it was a
long day at work but now I'm home and I'm so glad to see you. That's
what she wanted anyway dreaming about it about embrace which she
tried very hard to give other people but never felt herself. No arms
around this spirit. None at all. She pulled a chair out at the dining table
and read a little under fruit-bowl light fixture but no fruit in it save for
overripe lightbulb clicking with the age of a filament.

Daylight Monday. Seed finches exerting themselves from a shrub and
one was slower than the others he came last and with such obvious
effort his little paper wings. One week left after this one of June.

The Coroner said I have to show you this house. You're buying a house
the Father panicking where is it. Absolutely not it's empty in Palmyra.
Oh I think I know the one.

Walking to the empty house the Father thought of a return a son
coming home and suddenly people started springing up from the earth

surprise we've come back too. Would the son of god be startled when
this happened to him or would he expect it was the resurrection just
as frightening as the crucifixion. The Father's mother died before he
knew to return no one knew where to find him did he have a phone an
address was he alive didn't know the name of his university his seminary
finally Edna found in his mother's dresser drawer cleaning out her shirts
a billing statement from some school in Michigan called there found
him or evidence of him they knew where he worked relayed the news.
By then several months had passed and the Old Father died too. He
didn't know what of maybe grief or loneliness or anger. Mother dead of
ovarian cancer mutations in super-structural cells and tissues and vital
organs all spreading leaking through blood time and muscle. She said
no chemicals. Edna said she'd still had all her hair when she died and
wanted it that way and never once asked after her son even in pain.

Before she used to bring him hand in hand to the empty house
tend the garden there quietly chives and tomatoes and pepper plants no
one would ever know to harvest.

You think this place has anything to do with Shannon the Coroner
asked in an upstairs bedroom its purpose obvious only by whiter stain
on far wall where a headboard used to stand propped some glass and
drywall fluff on the floor crisp film for walking on. I don't think so
said the Father. She apparently comes here all the time. An empty
house doesn't explain the broadness of her situation. You're right I only
thought it'd be helpful. I wish it was.

Shading of leaves coming through shifting on the floor like animal
heads needing sleep dreaming.

The Coroner knew to be proper you had to practice tenderness.
Touching the Father's shirtsleeve. Hey. Yes I'm here. We'll find
something. Not here we won't. Okay not here but somewhere. Maybe
we won't. That'll be okay too. Will it be. Standing close now foreheads
glanced light coming through as between two mountains gold in
the afternoon and hot. The Father slighting away light opening up
a window-shaped leaf-filled hole on the floor we should go he said
moving to the door we should go. The Coroner trailing after looked
back into the room behind them as if the looked-for thing might want

apprehension in their absence a trick of the eye nothing there at all then suddenly.

When the Coroner returned to the Father's house. Went out the back door with a wicker basket balanced on his hip gathered eggs from the coop chickens pecked at his knuckles. Rubbed the eggs on front of his shirt getting the scat and dirt off. Shirt was white. Now stained. Total fourteen eggs some very warm in their post-birth skins. Returning through the door the Coroner asked the Father why hadn't he gathered eggs in a while. I've been preoccupied with thoughts. He set the eggs on the kitchen counter basket and all. What thoughts are preoccupying you. Same thoughts as always I suppose.

Hovering over the Father's house some spirit would see chickadees bobbing heads in the bushes struggling for posts upon which to stand upright wings half-stretched and hairy. Higher leaves in gutter roofing tiles awkward lying on top of one another weary and crooked and losing their corners to heavy wind here was the place where no eyes saw to correct fix or repair or care for. Higher the house diminished merely brown spot with darker chimney stack appended to it a field of green quilted stitched up golds and yellows and the combines moving through like slow dull-backed poisonous beetles. Higher and Palmyra's lean houses set into grass along the state route silently spectating cars higher Palmyra in the cornfields the unmade hay bales the horse stables Palmyra in the country in Ohio any higher than that and it's gone.

Edna walked through fields to reach beehives. Carrying a smoker in her left hand. Wearing the getup like a second skin face screened in. Just had to check on them for elderly neighbor Rudy not the first time she'd done it. Check to make sure they were doing alright. Height of summer good season for a honeybee. Good season for a person too but it was pretty hot in the bee suit.

Interior lining smelled like sweat dust pollen corn molds old man tobacco a little of her shampoo reflected back at her from her leaking

head. Pouring sweat down her forehead into her eyes under her chin but
she couldn't reach inside to wipe it off. Holding the smoker in her left
hand and screened in. In her other hand nothing. Swiping overgrown
grass away sometimes from her path Rudy put the beehives pretty far
out after one of Meredith's boys drove one over with a riding mower
chopping up the wood the frames the deep hive body the queen and
all the unfocused honey. Middle of summer three years ago must have
been. Shannon with Edna on the front porch hands on her hips mouth
slanted eyes hard just watching. A younger girl then but serious in all
she did. Edna stopped braced her free hand on her abdomen crouched
in the grass. Not tired or anything wanted to stop for a minute and be
quiet like she didn't even exist she couldn't see any houses or people
out here or nothing and closer now the subtle satisfied humming of
thousands of drunk bees rolling in one another's love. All warmed up.

Palmyra regretted her the former Father's wife in a way it had been
like excommunication if the Father returned but didn't want you. Must
be something wrong with the woman. Why in the first place did he
leave anyway but to run from her. She couldn't believe that. The Father
being a peculiar man but one unaccustomed to taking into account his
own wants and desires favorably over other people's she'd known him
all her life. If she'd asked him for anything he'd have given everything
he was resistant to giving. Must have been an outside force pressing or
calling him away maybe even god.

The wedding ring in her sock drawer in the velvet box it came in
same as the day he'd given it to her didn't even take a knee or nothing
handed her the box earnest eyes and a little afraid. She'd opened it. A
small silver band a single small stone belonged to my ma's ma he said
she gave it to me to give to you. Through high school they'd spoken
to one another seriously about starting families but that evening was
the first notion she'd had that he meant to start one with her of course
they'd kissed sometimes before then too they were teenagers and so
so isolated maybe the two loneliest people in the world definitely in
Palmyra. Naturally two solitary celestial bodies seek one another out.
Naturally do they fall into orbit and just as naturally she supposed do
they fall out but that never changed content mantle core or gravity.

Heel of her hand heavy on her hipbone now. It was this field he'd taken her to away from people finding them there was a sycamore at the end of it where trees broke up symmetry and held the dirt down before collapsing into another long field and she showed him how to climb that sycamore requiring upper body strength he didn't have. You can do it I'll help you so she gave him her hand and they pulled together. On the sloped upper limb the smallest that could hold both of them they peered through gaps in the leaves at piecemeal Palmyra talking about the things that melted their hearts down she wasn't very good with words failing English class and unable to audition for the school play Our Town as the Webb daughter even though she could've been good at it she had the lines memorized and everything so often the Father said for her what melted her heart or seemed to and all so correctly. She'd liked hearing those things spoken on air to her ears where she could hear them. Now she and the Father rarely spoke except politely and she was afraid she'd lost those things or was lost in them too big or too small for her to see anymore either completely gathering her soul up enveloping her and everything or half of a half of a grain of sand slipping secretly around in her lazy-river bloodstream no one would find it not even the Coroner when she died. No one would know to look except the Father and who knew if he would anymore. She liked to think so he still loved her somehow now that was confusing. She pushed herself up again rose from the grass continued on down the unmarked path to beehives.

I'm coming she said to no one but herself and the bees who were too far away at this point to hear exactly what she said. She heard them and not what they said too but she also didn't know their language. Vague low tinkling of insect wings and mouths. As she approached and beehives came into view long muttering rows of them like headstones she held out her right hand entreated with her approach for their meaning to show itself. The meaning did show itself she knew then that what they were saying was in fact singing and what they were singing was the song of what she'd lost.

Getting darker in the room as they talked and not turning lights on though the Coroner could reach behind his head feel the switch.

The Father squashed into little velvet armchair belonging once to his mother the Coroner across the room leaning on a stool he'd brought in from the kitchen shadows milky over angles of their faces making clear real sharpness in places light made hard to see. You know when she turns eighteen she's legally able said the Coroner. The Father asked legally able to do what. The Coroner said you know get an autopsy without you or Edna or her parents signing off first well not legally able more like it's just legal but I'll have her consent at the very least which is a strange circumstance for sure. That kind of scares me will it hurt her. No it won't hurt her. I just don't want it to hurt her. You're scared of her dying too aren't you. What do you mean. You're scared like Edna that she'll die and won't come back one day why is that.

The Father stared ahead eyes wide even across the room the Coroner saw the whites of them cupping his irises. Clasping his knees in both palms. I don't know what the world would be like without Shannon in it when the world is fighting so hard not to let her go. And you too. Huh. You don't know what the world would be like or you don't want to know. Both I think both. I think so too you're not just scared of men what is it you're really scared of. Lots of things I'm scared of water and climbing and men and women alike and myself and gunshots and god and him speaking to me and saying what I don't want to know you know all this. I do know but what is it behind all those things that you're scared of is what I don't know. I have no courage. Yes you do. I don't. The Coroner yawned not that he was bored but he was so tired and it was getting late. You do he said with finality and a little angry so the Father didn't argue it further. Will you come to bed with me he asked instead and the Coroner stood up stretched on his way out of the room.

In bed the Coroner embracing the Father's back flushly silent stiff-jointed and the Father said I'm sorry if I upset you. You didn't. Then why aren't you talking to me. The Father turned around so they lay face to face he examined the Coroner's contented mild apprehensive look with the side of his thumb and forefinger. He said there's something the matter please talk to me like you know you can I'm here to listen. I know but you won't talk to me. I do talk to you so often more than

I talk to anyone else even Shannon. Yes but you don't tell me things. I tell you things. Not the real things it's just in there I feel like I have to go in and draw it out myself but I'm not going to do that you know. Maybe you need to. No but I want you to trust me. I do. You might trust me more than you do other people but you still don't trust me I know you though better than you'd like me to. You're deep in my heart. I know. Really. I know.

The Father waiting for the Coroner to return his sentiments say something like you're deep in my heart too the home lodged in lungs yellow light waiting for filling and you're the one it fills for or like I care for you so deeply I would weave a net and wrap you in it silvery and thin as the smallest frailest spiderweb but strong enough to keep you safe and it's made of how much I love you but also afraid of the Coroner saying these things and knew how much the Coroner really felt them afraid of that too so glad the Coroner didn't say anything just closed his eyes pressed his temple to the Father's shoulder and eventually even slept.

Pie tin dance of earth's orbit man's orbit with all other men.

One green leaf held against Edna's screen by wind's dull barely feelable intake of breath. Shannon watching the leaf tremble tying her hair back with both hands before walking out the back door in the morning on her way to borrow a bike head to Gray for a while maybe antagonize Ian at the store counter and pinch her fingers in the binder he kept customers' addresses for deliveries in. Her face stretched out a little in window glass warped by early sunlight and age of superheated sand crystals talking back to her. Without finding shoes left the house first said goodbye to Edna in the kitchen and the Father and the Coroner on the Father's front porch leaning together like two tentpoles. So you two really depend on one another huh she wanted to call but didn't. What are you holding up she wanted to call but didn't she wanted to tell them there's no tarp hanging over your heads and

no rain to keep off your backs or like why don't you build a fire or
something to keep warm. Already a few steps outside she wiped sweat
from her armpits forehead and chest. To Meredith's garage where she
fetched the bike an old lemon yellow Huffy with a banana seat which
she had seen nowhere else but in movies as a kid. She guessed she still
was a kid sometimes.

She never took her time with things. Took a running start swung
onto the bike like some wild stallion-rider woman and pedaled hard
beating up the gravel berm. Several days later mysterious bruises would
appear on her legs where they hit against the metal bar big and purple
turning yellow fast. Most of her ride there totally flat but there was this
one big hill she hated putting effort into and she was trying to work
up enough momentum to conquer it which she did getting all the way
to the top without having to put much more speed down and then
at the bottom this field off the side of the road and in the field a path
recognizable so she stopped dismounted the Huffy rolled it into the
grass on its heaving flank.

Following the path for a while on the balls of her bare feet she came
into an ugly little cemetery the Father once showed her. This was long
ago early when she first arrived in Palmyra first met the Father. I don't
expect you to tell me about your circumstances he'd said and in some
ways I don't want you to I'd rather not have the burden of it now. Well
I wasn't gonna tell you so don't worry she'd said. I won't worry but I
wanted to tell someone anyway a little about mine if you don't mind.
I don't really want to listen neither. That's perfectly reasonable. She
thought then and now he was the saddest man on earth.

His parents were buried somewhere in this patch of woody rot-
smelling dirt both of them together right side by side. She kicked
around in the overgrowth trying to find some of them but found only a
fist-sized stone an old flower stand and one of Edna's relatives and some
poor woman unfortunate enough for the name Rose so she must have
been really old then not even a date carved into her some poor woman
named Rose with no birth or death only her name in a flat rock falling
over in the forest. Occurred to her suddenly that cremation solved
all their problems only she didn't really understand cremation very

well as an available concept having for someone who died so often a limited understanding of mortuary practice stemming from her limited understanding of scientific advancement outside amateur entomology and if approached about entomology in those terms she'd have thought oh they must be talking about the fact of her skin or something which she wouldn't have when she really died so why talk about it.

At Ian's store bought a strawberry fry pie from his bakery case with some money she found in her left shorts pocket and sat eating behind the counter Ian talking about some far-off imaginary place where he'd strike it big one day.

The night before Shannon's eighteenth birthday party. Earlier in the day the Coroner speaking to Shannon near the chicken coop by the lake said I guess it's morning now officially they were feeding the hens and a rooster crowed distantly. Shannon said the rooster crows cause he's awake not cause it's light out or anything he don't even know what the sun is. Extracting herself from a length of tendrily prehensile weed wrapped around her ankle. The little plant is taken by you said the Coroner laughing. No she said it's taking me. After feeding hens had a small dance party in the Father's kitchen cleaning up after themselves singing loud wrap your arms around me cover me. The Father came home from helping Edna with surprise preparations was startled by all the movement had to lay down for a minute on the couch close his eyes and just listen. They ate lunch with Shannon peanut butter honey sandwiches by the road then she went home wiping crust from the corners of her mouth with the back of her hand lurching as she walked. Big blue farmhouse stood open for her an open door and open windows.

Now the Coroner watched The Father watching the lake out a back window said we should go out there. The Father not answering. Really if we're checking things out. I don't know what the lake has anything to do with it said the Father finally. I know you're afraid but I'll be with you. I need some time to think about it. Okay you think about it then the Coroner went out to the backyard sat in the grass a little damp his pants and back soaking through after a few minutes. Flies like tracer bullets over the water picked off by bats or maybe night birds if those were such a thing the Coroner didn't know. A light in the Father's house making a yellow stain stretching longer than the window the Coroner tried taking it in his hand by a corner but couldn't peel it up off the grass stuck there a layer of creation.

The Father stepping outside sitting on the back stair with his head in his hands. Everything was so difficult lately. Messing up sermons more frequently forgetting so many words he knew. Afraid of keeping and afraid of losing but which one made him more afraid he didn't know they each meant something so heavy. Lifting his eyes from his palms to look upon the reclining Coroner in his yard in the grass washed partially in light from his house he felt a taut yanking pain drawing heart chambers and lungs together or maybe apart because there was so much space inside him for all the objects moments habits fears joys tumbling around to bump into one another in he wished for power enough to tie them down create firmament and waters and air but he was so small too small to contain a universe too small to create one and anyway he didn't know the words.

Do you live anywhere a voice came to him from his memory of the Old Father preaching several weeks before his leaving. I live in Palmyra Ohio he said aloud said it again again I live in Palmyra Ohio. The Coroner having heard half turned facing him in yellow profile features narrowed he hadn't known the Father was there. Of course you do he said. The Father a dark mass in the back doorway of the house blocklike long shadow.

Of course you do.

A square sheet cake white buttercream iced with images of insects. Her favorites as far as Edna knew to instruct the baker bee wasp which was longer than a bee beetle with black back dragonfly moth butterfly which was a sophisticated moth not one of Shannon's favorites but an understandable public favorite also a praying mantis and cicada larva. Picked out in blue lettering Happy 18th Shannon Wells. Bed of icing grass for the insects to play in. The cake sitting on Edna's dining room table suffused in pleasant light from an overhead fixture. Around noon people showed up helped decorate by two Palmyra had emptied itself into Edna's kitchen hanging streamers eating deviled eggs from a dainty plastic pink tray wanting the time to turn to five so Shannon would show up then eight precisely so they could go to bed.

Shannon not actually in Palmyra today she spent the day with Ian at the store and when he locked the doors he thrust keys at her. Do you still want a ride in that golf cart he asked. I probably do. Well you're eighteen now so you can even drive it you know. You're serious. Yeah I'm serious happy birthday Shannon. She tugged the keys from his hand took off running around back of the store kicking up earth where his family golf cart was locked up on a bike rack installed for that purpose. Tried three keys before finding one that fit in the bike lock got that off threw herself with commitment into the driver's seat Ian laughing pulling into the other side.

A slapped hand and a shaken finger don't touch those devilled eggs yet Robbie.

Blowing down little streets of Gray wind levelling her knotted hair down gathering speed. Make sure you don't get the brake pedal and gas pedal confused I made that mistake once and ran right through a glass door. I won't do that I'm no fool. When she was ten years old stole her mother's minivan ran right over black plastic mailbox at the end of their gravel drive the red flag dancing bent at a perfect ninety-degree angle by the collision across the street landing in the gutter. Done it on purpose even as a kid she knew what she was doing.

Young lady had her by the ear. Mother was a young lady. Bleach blonde with a ring through her lip a scar on her hip she'd fallen down the stairs in a laundry basket cut herself broke her daughter's leg that was when Shannon was three and she eighteen their birthdays almost fell on the same day. Missed it by seven and a half hours. Beautiful blue-eyed with her head out the car window. Saying in the night I love you my baby there's just enough room in my heart for one I can only ever love you.

Edna getting impatient it wasn't yet five. The Father found her put his hand on her shoulder she leaned in startled but safe. I haven't seen her since this morning but she'll be fine. That boy Ian better get her here on time. If he doesn't it won't be his fault. He moved past her for the bathroom.

Edna and the Coroner split with sameness in crowds two bodies pushing other bodies a few feet away from them with gravitational force. Hey would you like my hand was all it would take but they didn't see one another Edna busy laying out silverware the Coroner with his hands in his pockets leaned against a wall then touching his lips with the tips of his left pointer index middle fingers seeming very far away and the Father in front of the mirror pressing his forehead solid against the tired forehead of his other self.

Heading for Palmyra at a gusty twenty-five miles per hour. Breaking free of Gray brick-faced and linoleum storefronts lopped off all at once the ends of them wrapped in summer ivy touched gold in fading day getting close to five now Ian checked his watch. It was the road the strip of flat asphalt-burned grass before the corn-tall world it was nothing but corn out there under a great big blue halo a tiny eye turning orange. They passed the place where corn ceded to grass and the path toward the cemetery. Shannon and Ian not speaking or looking at one another. Palmyra's crooked rebar sign. Ian finally said can you stop here a minute. Shannon tearing at the brakes both bodies colliding briefly hard with the dashboard. Recovering themselves. Do you want to go to the house real quick. Shannon shrugged sure as long as I drive. He agreed so they cut through the first lawn two narrow tire impressions in grass diminishing until taller grass swallowed up and separated for them. To maneuver the cart through woodland was more difficult but Shannon managed listening minimally to Ian's guidance.

In the house both leaning out a second story window looking at an evening shadow pooling underneath its inky yellow humors.

Ian touched her elbow. She turned. You have nice skin. I can't tan ever it always just burns not that I'd want to tan anyway. He put pressure on her elbow drawing her into himself feeling curve of another stomach warm beneath t-shirt sweat wetted. Hot in the abandoned house some stale air circulating on the floor a tender brown leaf. He kissed her a little sloppy moist upper lip unpracticed even getting inside her mouth before she open-handed hit his neck blowing the breath from him she jumped back.

I told you I don't like boys. I'm not one. I don't like men neither I don't like nobody that way. You kissed me back. I ain't sorry but it did suck. She began to cry. Shannon what's wrong the weight of a broad hand on her back another on her shoulder. I'm dead Ian. You mean like you got the cancer. No I mean what I said I'm dead already I've died.

At six-thirty Edna really worried now. Asked the Coroner if she should call the police. He didn't know what for she was a wild child and prone to lateness anyway you couldn't put in a missing persons report until twenty-four hours after which did nothing to calm her. The Father with his mouth on a glass of water paused mid-sip didn't resume drinking put glass down watched its bioluminescent shadow wiggle over top of his hand gripping the counter. Lots of people trying to make small talk about weather with him or reminisce over days of the Old Father and his mother. Remember your birthday party forty years ago and your mother made this cake shaped like a dog with a little pink nose and you hadn't wanted to eat him no you wanted to keep him all in one piece as cute as he was. I remember it but I barely remember it. I was there your mother wore her white dress. I remember the wind blowing under it. You have your mother's cheeks nose and eyebrows and your father's temperament. If there was one thing for certain he prayed for it was for that not to be true. He was tempered neither like his mother nor the Old Father he rather thought in terms of temperament he conformed to the place he was in. The soil of Palmyra crying against its beloved people and the people against it but they would never move one another would they just lie on top of one another eternally tired not sleeping turning over with dreams of what tremors what movement was it transubstantiation then. Was it the transformed face of the land.

Then it was the hour of darkness someone called Shannon is coming so Edna turned out the lights lit two candles lopsided on the cake stood before it a set-apart woman made of shadows like a paper doll. Shannon entered quietly through the front door stopping letting her eyes adjust to a new dimness. Surprise. Shouted again when she didn't react surprise faltering at the tail. In meager light they could see one dark cut below her left temple strapping her chin coming to her right cheek. Dusty complexion puffy skin dirt sticking to undersides of her red eyelids. Oh god said Edna. The Father looking horrified not for her condition but for some tender realization fallen on him all of a sudden. Shannon gripping a limb-thick walnut branch in right hand. How long you been sitting here waiting for me she asked not waiting herself for an answer just walking through a part in the crowd to the cake table where Edna stood matchbox still in hand. Shannon observing the cake in the twin candle glow. Laying the branch on the floor at her feet bracing strong arms on the edge of the table leaning in feeling small growing heat on her nose turned down her head blew out the candles and navigated the full room in full darkness immediately upstairs to bed.

Some well-oiled sadness this was. Shannon's dream of an ocean growing up to swallow the earth and Palmyra in one and somewhere up there the Father in the sun.

The Father and the Coroner were going together to Robbie Lou's green canoe moored to a dock overgrown with reeds Robbie Lou believed real fishermen only used boats in emergencies and so far this year no emergencies yet. The knot holding the canoe to the dock when they found it with their hands was the same knot from last year possibly too the year before that. The Coroner having to cut it away with his pocketknife one of the few knives sharper than butter in Palmyra not locked in a case.

He held out his hand for the Father standing unfounded a little way from where the reeds began. It's okay he said just a little buggy you might get bit up. I'm not worried about mosquitoes in the least. I'm right here. I know. The Coroner entering the canoe first from the back helping the Father down into the rowing seat. I'm going to steer all you have to do is row switch sides every now and then. I know how to row a canoe. I know you do.

Setting out the Coroner keeping eyes on folds in the Father's shirt steadying himself with the back oar steering their way to the center of the lake. The Father not an exceptional rower but decent enough for propulsion. The Coroner didn't need to goad him into deepness. So they went into the center of the lake didn't really know what they looked for could be anything like an invisible sense of gravity or a skater bug didn't know what those were called really but the Coroner knew Shannon knew and suddenly wished he'd brought her along instead. Wait not instead but along with of course he wanted the Father with him here though silent stiff difficult to plumb and altogether closed up. Hey said the Coroner. The Father startled dropped his oar a solid slap of wood on sturdy water. I have to tell you something. The Father asked what do you have to tell. Before I tell you do you believe in the whole walking on water thing. What walking on water thing are you talking about. You're a preacher you should know. Oh in the Bible I guess I do believe in walking on water I have to but people have only ever tread water once or twice so don't you try it now please. I'd like to test a hypothesis of faith though it's scientific I promise and it will only take a minute and if it works I'll believe in god. I'd rather you didn't honest. The Coroner lifted to his feet in the back of the canoe swaying over small resulting waves and the Father too terrified to turn around and see a splash drip and the Coroner was in the water and after a while didn't resurface for breath or a joke or anything and the Father still not turning didn't know what to do if he should dive headlong in or wait for the worst to happen as undoubtedly it would the worst always being more likely to happen the longer he resisted it.

Okay this isn't funny he said to no one on the surface at all then he said just as loud I'm really afraid. That was when the Coroner decided to come back up slapped his hands against the side of the canoe to climb aboard and the Father capsized under the water. It had been a long time. Breathe.

Pulling the Father back to shore required first locating him underwater getting a good grip not on his shirt but top of his arm where muscle met bone figuring a way to swim nearly quarter of a mile attached to another person in this way who quite frankly wasn't assisting at all in urgency or salvific efforts. So the Coroner did this swallowing a little water but when he beached them both first himself then tugging the Father ashore behind him the Father was the one to throw up then he sat on his knees and cried heavier than when he was a child and didn't understand how to properly cry and understand too what he was crying for which was the unreboundable sorrow of being a person and oftentimes not knowing how to say so. Bent the reeds around them by the wind a shelter from being seen there being sad about it.

Rising unsteadily from the reedbed toward the shrouded glow illuminating windows of his far-off house drawing near to the back door turned and without looking pressed together until their bodies formed one molded silhouette stark against lake and light. Both so spent from the swim and the walk their knees quaked together as they folded in.

What did you see down there asked the Coroner. I saw well I wasn't really thinking I couldn't see anything outside my own head. This was untrue he saw all creation knuckle-ridged before him a fearsome vision. Did you ever see god. I haven't seen him not tonight not ever but once I don't know I want to see him if I'm able I'm not ready to. You're right I understand what you're saying.

The Coroner understood more than he admitted but now was not the time to scare the Father with such images because he'd seen god in the water or what god there ever was all brown silt and suspended matter and a floor of moving sand an atmosphere thick so his arms left

pockets of air behind when he moved them. Standing in the Father's
yard he felt none of that same wonder he skimmed the curved brow of it
a thin vein of lightning whipping through the clouds turned the Father's
bowed head white. The Coroner touched his hair where it had shone.

They went inside. For the rest of the night not talking except to ask
where things were. The Coroner borrowing a button-down shirt from
the dryer he toweled himself off sitting next to the Father on the couch
even when he flinched.

Before dawn he sighed and said that he should leave and the Father
nodded mutely. The Coroner wore a pale consternation which was as
borrowed from the Father as the shirt. He asked do you love me.

The Father. Couldn't answer right away. Earlier ghosting through
halls he'd caught the Coroner squeezing water from his hair off the side
of his porch door half-open head thrown over the rail feet bare and
curled against the wood and he loved him so much then he thought his
throat would burst from holding it in so satisfying and shocking that a
man existed outside himself who adjusted perfectly to his maladapted
life who walked with him shoulder to shoulder who marveled at the
crown of his head. Yes he said. Do you really. Yes yes I do. You love me.
Yes of course I love you. Will you live with me. What did you just say. I
said will you live with me or I understand that's maybe asking too much
I would be willing to live with you the drive to work doesn't bother me
honestly and you can think about it but I love you and I do want to be
with you possibly for the remainder of my life. I will have to think about
this. That's okay I want you to. I'm sorry. Don't be sorry just think about
it seriously. Okay. I should go. I guess so.

Walking him to the front door the Father wanted to kiss him
but couldn't in his head form the commands required for simple
actions when he thought they came to him overblown in some areas
undergrown in others they came to him in collapsing piling tumoroid
shapes half-envisioned creatures from primordial stew always turning to
show him some new side even less formed than the last. He was afraid
if he reached out his hand it might swell to the size of a watermelon
if he touched the Coroner's face it might shrink down to the size of
a grape tomato and roll away if he touched the Coroner's lips to his

who was to say who would slide through and who would keep going
and who was to say one would not swallow the other because they'd
gotten so big and the other so small and it was only an accident he
would say but it wouldn't matter. He was full of accidents he would
hold in his body until they became him. He was Edna and Shannon
and the Coroner all loving him being loved by him being lonely with
him because of him he was his Old Father his mother his unborn upset
children terrorized by their progenitor's sorrow he was the belief in god
and wishing god wasn't true he was and he wished
    since his second birth
    he wasn't.

He got away with excusing his behavior imagining Palmyra all there was
in the world and the lake the world's only ocean and in a very individual
sense this was true individual speaking directly to the individuals of
Palmyra most of whom had never walked past Gray because other than
Gray and the eventual ocean there was little else living out there. What
mattered to them beyond the vastness. They possessed it all on the broad
brows of hills and geese carried it sometimes in with them spreading it
over shingles and lake water under fat wings fat with stories of distance
and longing and knowing in summer where was safe to come back to
where family could spring up spontaneously from the formless earth
where all guaranteed loving you with plenty through no absence of
misunderstandings but at least their eyes tried to see and whatever they
saw was loved most of all. I mean it said the Coroner before leaving.
So maybe this place had absorbed covered even him too or maybe not
maybe not. What if all spoken word was in a sense true. What if there
was a true spoken word for every man woman and child. What if the
truth was this place and this place rousing itself from the sleep of death
over again and over again pressed deep as wax seals into their bodies.
Everyone started to look the same to him. Frightening resemblance away
he'd only frighten himself into not believing.

———

What would it be like to finally be home to enter into belonging someplace truly belonging. She figured sort of like stepping out of a taxi it was a sliver of nighttime coolness buried in the earth she toppled it over with her step a big blue farmhouse rising from a soft split body an upper light on but the lower windows dark as if all were sleeping inside and front door open with the screen door shut nothing no luggage no bags no burdens not even any clothes just the first step out of a taxi from an old life into the next one edges of grass blades crushed itchy between her toes damp in autumn. It would be like that exactly like that and nothing else for her. It would be like a hole in the middle of a planet where a lake lived and in the lake swam voices of all the people who loved her and whom she loved so deeply because of their ridiculous irrational loving.

The Father slept two days developed a fever turned him pale flashed fire through his body he sweated through sheets he curled into a tight ball a pill bug on his cool floor and squeezed his eyes shut but he felt his soul had departed from him and hovered a few inches around his skin. He itched his arms raw trying to throw it off.

It was Palmyra it was this place bearing down on him but he knew that wasn't really true. He liked to fool himself. He liked to think that if he danced in widening circles eventually his little paternal faith would encompass all aspects of everyone he loved and who loved him and even himself and there would be no madness or jealousy or fracturing of the spirit in that mythical place that healed him whole. How he longed for heaven how he feared he'd never see it. His reaching it he felt required more sacrifice than his body tolerated giving or else some incredible gymnastic act a balancing on one pedestal then another until his legs grew so tired he collapsed and fell five-hundred feet to a concrete floor. Life afforded no safety nets no trampolines or resets though this was a difficult claim to justify in light of what happened in Palmyra.

He did not call the Coroner the following day instead stayed home and dreamed that he would he lay in bed playing over an outstanding fantasy in which he gave up his ghosts in the country and walked a long way by the road and the Coroner eventually found him in his car with its rattling engine and the smell of oil dripping onto the heating coils coming through the air vents and he said everything's waiting for you and they drove to the city and the Father imagined this part in real time so that an hour after lying down he arrived in the city and he imagined his life there sitting in coffee shops with glass window fronts and baristas that knew your order but not your name and he picked out a modern sofa for their new apartment and he picked out a new job at one of those call centers until one day he got a call from Shannon Wells and he cried and the one in charge fired him and the world fell apart windows poured from buildings buildings sunk under the ground and he was lying in bed. The crickets played sad strings of silence through his walls. Shadowed antlers crossed his bedroom as a herd of deer traveled south through Palmyra looking for the right kind of grass to sleep. When he went to sleep the sun had yet to set completely behind the soy and cornfields and the lake and he dreamt something else. He dreamt his massive dream of sleeping in the sun.

Shannon and Ian no longer speaking. Which she found unfortunate owing to the fact she did a little like him at least his company and then there was the Father who hadn't come over for breakfast or brunch three mornings in a row. I'll go talk to him Shannon told Edna the end of the fourth morning. Coming close to Sunday now and they'd need him. Edna scooping uneaten fruit into paper bag for compost pile in the backyard. Okay she said seeming like she meant it from a million miles away she was thinking actually about the garden they'd never had together because there wasn't time. In everything she'd wished for more time so when eternity came Edna knew exactly what she'd do with it now wouldn't she and that was a comfort.

Shannon didn't bother with shoes or new clothes she'd slept in her work clothes from day previous pruning Meredith's garden for her because she had four children to take care of and a husband who farmed for a living so a pruned garden was important. Was paid twenty dollars for it probably too much but the garden was bigger than average with a rickety wire fence to keep rabbits out and a rickety wire house William and Bethany's 4-H rabbits sometimes got out of. In bib overalls and a grubby white t-shirt then the same t-shirt for the whole week Edna hadn't bothered her about a shower yet so Shannon smelled a little like manure and sphagnum and peppers. The Father's door was open she went in didn't find him in the study didn't find him in the living room lying across the fullness of his couch with his elbows over his eyes like sometimes he did or in the kitchen staring out the window and no one in the bathroom. Did find him in the bedroom on the floor bedsheet pulled from the bed around his shoulders she could only see him by his shape. Went in kicked his shoulder roughly. Hey you what do you think you're doing laying around like some lump. Shannon I'm not feeling well right now. If you're so sick you should've told someone. You wouldn't. No I sure wouldn't but you're not me so you should be smarter and act like a man. Sometimes I wish I weren't one like you might wish not to exist. That's not what I wish for. Isn't it. No and you don't know me as well as you want to so don't go around thinking you do. Are you mad at me. Yes.

She crouched near his head lifted the bedsheet put her spare hand on the sweaty crown of his head dark and shining. You're sure sick she said but I don't mean it like an illness your illness is like something you imagine in you. Or something I hold in me I need to go away. That won't help nothing and you know it you go as far as you like but if it's in you then nothing goes trust me. You don't really want to exist do you. Fuck you really I do.

I don't know how.

Me neither but I do and I keep existing and I better get used to it someday even when it hurts until one day it doesn't and I don't exist anymore but I don't think that day'll ever come death ain't not existing.

I know.

You don't she said but he did and what happened when he still existed frightened him most of all so he stopped talking and drew his arms over his head cutting her off from touch she lowered the bedsheet placed her bare foot over his back barely touching him and his cowering coveredness went back to Edna's home the blue farmhouse.

Edna dropped her dishes alarmed at the shaking walls the door slammed suddenly then Shannon in the kitchen. I can't stay she said so with finality. What happened and just where do you suppose you'll go miss. I can't stay here.

Edna looked her up and down conflicted painful face felt it in her tightened features not another time she thought this little love too leaving. Wanted to reach her hand out and for Shannon to take it. Wanted to hug her clutch her close impossible against leaving anything but that. When she loved her so much like her own daughter from a lonely womb daughter she never chanced to have due to the Father's unwillingness. Not unwillingness she corrected herself the Father's distance his spirit caged up for her unreachable incapable as they were of feeling right with only one another and happy and unlonely too. Oh but she had been those things. She saw Shannon her little gray eyes full of all the world's uncertainties pink wet face had she been crying she felt her own neck close up no this couldn't be but she had to love her still. And always.

Alright she said go on and pack your things I'll help you with a cab and get you out of here.

When she first arrived those years ago delinquent the image of a snake sliding through Palmyra gardens uprooting vegetables or eating them or shoving fistfuls of thoroughwort into her shorts pockets stem by stem by stem by stem. Smelling like snapped thoroughwort.

No one had expected her. Small girl in her goldenness. She carried wads of loose paper money with her in a duffel when she got out of the cab and she'd hidden it someplace in Edna's attic Edna didn't try to look for where. Thought maybe her life had gone sour and she needed most of all not to be found in anything or for anything of hers to be found. So let it alone. Shannon spent the first week of her residence in Palmyra in isolation running out across the hills beyond her neighbors' worry. Gradually kept closer to home. But neighbors started wishing she took up wandering again on account of how she got into everything embedded her body and hands in their business their lives their peace. Unintentional. She was just a girl.

She got seen by Robbie Lou the first time snatching eggs from a robin's tree nearly fell twenty odd feet to the hard unfarmed earth where the roots grabbed it and would've cracked her collarbone. He hollered at her across from his canoe. In just his galoshes and jeans and his long prewar hair tied back. Where's your daddy child he hollered like a dog. She caught herself on a caddy-corner branch caught the eggs in her hand managing unstunned to break none of the two of them.

I don't got none she hollered back to prove she had a dog's bark too. He sat at the back of his canoe petting his beard. You say you got none now where you from child that's no Ohio voice. You don't got to know about where I come from mister. But you say you got no daddy. Naw but I sure got me a Father. If that ain't the truth Robbie snuffed his nose and spit into the water. It was the truth from the start. She had her a Father.

The Father then. While Rob insisted she unfurl her hand and they marveled at her delicate blue miracles leaning together like Christ and the sinner in lines of her calloused palms he had his eyes and mind turned to other mandates not only Lazarus come forth and the loosing and letting go of graveclothes but also ye bring forth abundantly in the earth and multiply therein the contexts of those verses occluding like an earlier than anticipated dawn in the corners of his vision. Drawn his blinds and shut his windows firmly locked them too against the wind or whatever other prying forces sought to destroy his most private darks. Sweat scaled piling on the forehead effort extracting it from the skin a drawing out of all evil. Slow the force and tide of movement bodily all. Please go slowly he told the Coroner's ear slower it was all he could do most days to breathe. Staring long at the ceiling fan could sometimes turn her backward. He hoped it was like that with time. The Coroner bent his legs to his chest.

Oh oh no. Mouth on rib bone pulling it out separating the water of himself from the water of himself what wheat from what chaff the great winnowing would happen one day in the field now that it was nearly October crops started vanishing into collection trucks for dispersement. The fire of weaving through a body. The invoked name of god. The invoked name of the Father. The time he skinned his knee as a child and had to be held to cease his wailing. The first he touched the back of a bird how the feathers rebounded like foamy cake. The spun around and dizziness of being in arms. The wanting to be in arms. The holding tighter. The fire of weaving through a body. He breathed. The fire what he felt the astonishing interior heat of the fire. Massive dream of sleeping in the sun.

He kept the Coroner close to his chest even when the fire had gone extinguished itself completely in his gut and legs and unwound shoulder blades the aching region of his thigh where the Coroner had grabbed him to support himself. Would bruise in an hour dark storm cloud stain migrating its colors as it healed.

Not looking at him nor raising his head from the Father's crazy grasping the Coroner touched his face. Round of his jawbone hem of an ear soft hill of cheek tender eye corner velvet ridge of brow lesson of the forehead. Wet sweaty. Skated his fingers.

I'm trying to remember you. The Father in silence. Not that I'm afraid of forgetting really but I want to remember you now the way you are now. Like an injured animal maybe he didn't know what to say.

Another recalled sensation the one of wanting to weep at beautiful things. He said finally the Father said you make me want to cry. I didn't hurt you did I. No. I really tried to be careful and do this right for you. I feel great you're wonderful. The Coroner on a big sigh answered that he agreed on both how great how wonderful. The Father's body wanting to cry but not bringing itself to the fullness of it. He rolled the Coroner onto his back you're so beautiful he said his forehead pressed anxious to his sternum you're so beautiful.

Shannon never intended to eat the eggs nor smother them nor crease and crack their baby thin shells wanting of course only to hold them

hot of some guardian body though the guardian absent watching from
some other distant crook. High up certainly. And had he been absent
since the hour she arrived.

Robbie Lou showed her to put the eggs back holding her
forearm tight in one hand against her struggle to flee from this new
responsibility thrust upon her and the other gently letting the twins
tumble back to lay in their nest secure. But not safe he said the mammy
mightn't want these babies cause of you Shannon now what do you say
to that. She said nothing. Gave him grim darting little threats with her
face as he dropped her went back to his work at the fishing shed finally
prying off the door removed a gun from his back pocket and weighed
it sure as the first anxiety in his grip. Then she watched him lock it in a
firesafe underneath some paint-spattered sawhorse.

It wasn't until three months later Robbie Lou noticed the gun was
gone his father's pistol he used to kill fish sometimes a single shot to the
head you're dead.

In the evening didn't matter what the day was like thick pastes of rain
or sun of weightlessness the spirillic whistle of late summer birds. Or in
the spring when the light went down to sleep golden on oak branches
hung heavy already with the little amber eyes of unborn leaves. Soon to
arrive and small because of it. The quality of light yellow like a steno pad
reminded him of his childhood there was a certain game he and some
neighbor boys played. A frisbee would be thrown and all would stumble
after it purposefully sliding to their knees to see at the end of the day whose
jeans could dye greener. Sometimes wading into the lake they'd try to
catch fish in their teeth like in fiction. He imagined the real slide of scales
between exposed bone the falling slimed ridges of fish skin struggling on
his tongue the taste of ache mire and tang of silver color. If he had ever
actually caught one. He hadn't. Nobody had not even those who waited
in their father's galoshes and camouflage pants with their heads bent down
perpendicular to the water an eye for movement. Nothing came to those
who'd wait. Except the light would change and evening would come and
the birds started up again their warning sleep calls.

This evening the Father considered choices in his lifetime which may or may not have concluded with his current moment his current deep buried sadness. Most of all early conversations with the Coroner and the Coroner asking one evening several years ago like this one in the name of transparency I have to ask why are you so angry with me. Both sitting in Edna's library she'd left to get tea made this look like sheets of bare paper. The Father at first said nothing. Seriously the Coroner said what did I do to piss you off so bad if you're a righteous man it must be righteous anger right. I'm not angry at you. That was the choice he made. What then. I'm not angry I'm sorry I'm being unjustly cruel to you it's because I'm conflicted between my feelings and my spirit. The Coroner seemed to softly understand that. What conflict.

Then there was ever leaving Palmyra he considered also if it ever was a choice. His mother making vital phone calls by the kitchen window late at night where suddenly it became early in the day. What kind of person would he be then. Sunken wet saying no I don't want to go.

A crack of fire through the air. The Father upright immediately clutching his ribs screaming. Oh god don't do this please dear lord but when he looked around there was no one there he leaned back against the carpet tried to remember how to breathe. How to. Do whatever. The phone rang he couldn't answer it he still didn't have any answers he missed the Coroner too much wanted him too much so he knew already what decision that would make him. And anyway he didn't deserve to hear good voices. When it occurred to him what had actually happened he horrified ran across the route to the farmhouse almost run over by a buggy without flashers but what was another black horse anyway.

Despite growing pain in her abdomen Shannon managed to pull herself to the telephone call the Father's house. She tried to remember did he have a phone. The first time it went to answering machine she tried again the Coroner's number he answered how convenient she gasped I think my kidney's broke and she blacked out.

At Edna's when the Coroner arrived the Father and Edna already in the stairwell Edna weeping on the Father's shoulder and the Father just sitting there letting his shoulder soak up her weeping. The Coroner took them up to Shannon had the Father hold her side where it bled. No tighter really. I'm hurting her. No you're not you can't hurt her anymore right now you have to really hold tight or she'll bleed out and die do you hear me tighter until the blood barely gets through your fingers. Okay okay. Are you scared. Yes. It's okay hold together. I'm trying do you see me goddammit I'm trying. The Coroner touching the Father's shoulder saying I know you are quietly before withdrawing from the room. Came back with Edna and a floral bedsheet. We're going to move her onto this then down the stairs into my car keep holding on. So the Father kept holding.

On the way to the hospital stretched head to toe in the backseat of the Coroner's sedan knees bent a little to make room the Father sat folded between the driver's seat and the floor weeping stroking her hair grasping her hip oh god. The Coroner cut the backroads at ninety-seven miles an hour. Sharp wedges of light tearing away darkness. Revealing scrub weeds gullet on side of road dead deer hidden driveway. Edna at home wringing her hands together though she had no way of knowing.

I'm stopping here. The Coroner almost hit a mailbox corkscrewing into a gravel drive. He idled the car. So the lights were still on little yellow spot they watched for Shannon to stop breathing and eventually she did. He rolled down a window cool and full. Checked the time.

He asked should I call the office and arrange an autopsy. The Father didn't answer and the Coroner knew he wouldn't he shouldn't have even asked. Okay then that's the way it is. Turned the car around headed back for Palmyra. Rocking the Father Shannon's body the interior of the car a burning smell as oil dripped onto heating coils. There was quiet weeping and the Father still held on and the blood slowed a little but not much. Back at Edna's blue farmhouse parked in the grass the Coroner opened the back passenger door asked the Father to please move over the Father didn't and had to be pulled gently from the car and would you like to have something helpful to do or would you rather be on your own for a while and the Father still didn't

answer so the Coroner went in asked Edna for tweezers sewing needle
and fine thread himself also more towels and I think you should come
out pick him up and get him to wash his hands if you want something
to do yourself. So she did retrieve those things the Father last of all
bringing him into the house forcing him into the bathroom bowing
him over the tub hot water poured over his hands from a glass she
kept by the sink for late-night spitting but she did wash it first. Ghosts
of Shannon's blood down the drain. Red lines connecting him to a
sewer system somewhere. Sulfuric tang of well-begat water stuck in his
nostrils. Receding to a middle spot in himself what floated in water
what sank. Leaning over ribs hurt.

Okay Edna said you're clean and when he held his hands out for
more she poured a finally filled glass over his head.

I do deserve that.

I know you do.

It's my fault this time for certain she's dead and I ain't going to run
from that.

That's not what it was for.

You tell me what it was for then Ed.

It was for to clean you.

You're trying to absolve or baptize me now.

No I just wanted you to know for a long long time that I do really
forgive you and love you all the same whatever that means to you and I
don't feel entirely that my life now is your fault but I known a lot of it is
and for that it's okay you should know I forgave you soon as you done it.

His mouth was dry he said are you sure that's true.

Can't not be to me but I suppose you might feel differently.

Ed I'm so so sorry I'm so sorry for everything.

There ain't no way you can really fix it what you carry around
been inside you since we were just little together so if you're sorry
feel sorry for yourself then do something about it really. Setting
the cup down at the bottom of the tub she lay a hand on his head
kissed his head through the top of her hand and there was a hope of
transference in the gesture that shocked the both of them and she
had to leave the bathroom him alone wondering at what didn't feel so

good wondering at what was heavy and where he would find arms to keep carrying it.

The Coroner had to go back inside for scissors once before starting. Hadn't realized how deep and clean the wound was and a little inexperienced in making cuts on those you might expect to have to live a long time with them so he wanted to be careful. Found some alcohol too because you never know what the dead feel. When he drew the bullet out he rolled it shiny on the hem of his shirt weighed it in the palm of his hand. He left the blue farmhouse he left his car he left Shannon in the car he left the doors open but he brought the bullet with him.

The Father watched her waiting for any sign of real resurrection or that christ or someone might rise from her body like a ghost and tell him what the meaning of all this was why these cycles why this why him why her. Death seemed irredeemable to him even as a child he'd watched the Old Father put a sick hen on an oak stump levelling its head under his palm cleaving its neck with a knife from the house and for a minute the hen could still have been alive the knife making way for the shape of its neck curving around then the blood began to pour and spritz he ran in the house tucked himself behind the couch stared at floral wallpaper parallel lines of blue baby blooms for several hours. Then ten years later on Old Father's bedroom floor feeling a pressure mounting in his lungs the same wallpaper throughout the house the first thing he'd torn away when he moved in again then he'd taken out the old bed but most other things he became frightened of and left alone.

Sitting close to morning on Edna's front stair alone drying from being washed the Father bowed his head. In times of grief or shame he always bowed his head a pedagogical ritual and the only one he knew. It was so complicated when wanting things so badly could rend him from four decades of living that he could never go back to again and what should he pray for. His body trying to collapse in on itself. So tired. He went across the street home.

In the foyer he removed his shoes stood quiet in the sepulcher dark hallway looking to the kitchen where the little light over the sink was on. In the yellowness of the light the Coroner moved back and forth between the sink and coffeemaker occasionally stopping to work at the dishes that had accumulated there over the course of the week and the Father felt not for the first time the divine notion that he lacked the right to intercede. He wanted to go in he wanted to help dry plates and silverware with the white rag hanging over the handle of the oven ask the Coroner how was his day kiss his ear receive call and response. He wanted to say no one died in Palmyra Ohio but even when death walked backwards through time he felt its bright head lie down on his shoulders he felt fear he felt sorrow he felt that nothing could be negated nor taken back. He wanted to go in. He wanted the Coroner and Shannon and god simultaneously.

He stood in the hallway until the Coroner saw him stepped a little closer until only a foot divided them like approaching an animal. The Coroner said are you lonely sometimes. Yes I am so so lonely sometimes no all the time I am suffused in loneliness I mean it's really diffusing in me like some arterial clog dissolved and gone out through my blood but it doesn't leave me it stays in my whole body I'm so lonely. I can't help you not feel it but believe that you're not alone. I do. You don't really know it. I'm trying to it's difficult. I know.

Bowing his head to the Father's shoulder slow the Coroner took up a learned posture of prayer or young slow dancing one hand planar on the Father's lower neck the other pressed on the contoured round of his cheek drawn in drawn down to twoness. Their breath came and went from the same slotted space they stole it sometimes from each other all warmth and bread and sharpness. Eyes closed I love you I love you okay okay okay.

He could not tolerate such a separation of his parts god created men as he created the heavens seven days before he created them men and women he created them scattered through the blackness of the universe with room to expand but no company and whose job was it to tend to the emptiness between glowing bodies whose dominion was that whose cross to bear whose impossible urgent task and his heart crushed him as it collapsed. The Coroner held him tighter. He'd felt the reverberations of massive stars forming somewhere far away wanted to fold him under an embrace spanning the distance and time of eternity. You're not alone.

Shannon's dream when she was dead. Someone with warm wet hands touching her hair pleasing out knots with pleasurable pressure leaving in the ones she wanted. A voice close to her lips on the edge of her ear. Wake up again if you want to wake up or even if you don't. This world is the other one so if you think this is hell now you'll have to learn an eternity of patience alright and the voice was comforting somehow though she would forget it when she rose again maybe her mother's young before children but her womb open for them just one in particular already knowing her. She would also forget the other pair of hands hugging her middle and the other pair of hands holding her own closing around them like a passed-down jewelry clasp so firm and so tight so impossible to let go.

He angled the Father's head between his chest and shoulder. They spoke quietly with the lights on in the manner all great secrets were divulged before the makers let the world choose form.

It did hurt when he was shot. He told the Coroner this. The Coroner slid his hand underneath the Father's shirt four fingers flat against his middle right rib looking to the Father for confirmation and the Father shook his head and moved the fingers to the other side. Perfected in love perfection in love something like that. He could count this life as his only one. The first one. If only he could cut the rest of himself off but he couldn't. The shot to his lung was not immediately fatal. He died of shock and blood loss and eventually asphyxiation. While he died the Old Father talked to him stroking his arms. I will lead you through this and you will see the face of god and he will judge

whether you're right or wrong. Meanwhile a fear permeating the dim
bedroom swollen blood-tasting tongue teeth he could no longer feel
and airways suddenly aching from his awareness of them. Hidden
nerves constricting. Panic as the Old Father closed his eyes and he
could not open them again there was no command to make them open
how to open how to how. Flower scent of garden yellow cup of petal
overfilling with rain wax on skin skin broken as something else sealed
his bones and then nothing.

The Old Father folded his son into a black trash bag with a
cinderblock. He rowed out to the middle of the lake and slid him in.
He watched his son's formlessness diminish into black-and-brownness
then only brownness and the faintest reflection of canoe and weeping
man with oar crowned in starlight. He thought this is the way the first
father must always baptize the second. He rowed home. By his bedside
in the blood thanking the lord for the life of his son and praying for
forgiveness at having taken it and god forgave him and the god who
forgave him was perfect and the god who forgave him was problematic
and the god who forgave him had no desire for these discrepancies to
be understood.

It was close to morning and Edna saw the lights still burning in the
Father's house across the road set hard against Palmyra's navy-hilled
horizon like some prop in a school play. She'd had her role in it
this time round at least and maybe she'd get another but relieved it
wouldn't be the same one felt a ribbon tugging loose and letting go
at the exact center of her chest. Releasing radial lifetimes of pain. She
thought of honey pouring from severed comb and of pictures she'd
seen in Shannon's thesaurus of flares arcing loose from the sun cosmic
superheated double-dutching in space and it was difficult to believe in
but she was used to these things coming along with difficulty like a goat
tied to a long rope. Well. And because the word love was close to her
newly unfastened heart she got to worrying again about Shannon Wells
up in her attic climbed upstairs immediately to check on her.

She was awake in bed blinking fast and fast sat up when Edna came close pulled herself carefully onto the sheets. Do you know what time it is Shannon asked Edna and Shannon said no I don't know what time is it. It doesn't much matter close to sunrise I suppose. Sounds alright by me. Will you still be needing that ride out of here I'll bet the Coroner might be convinced to take you to town for free. No if it's alright I think I've changed my mind for now but. But. I don't know just but. You look tired Shannon. I am but I don't think I could sleep right this minute not even if all the night in the whole world broke all your windows and knocked me flat out.

Edna reached forward without thinking and touched the child's hair pure desire ancient reflex and Shannon never brushed it so strong was its call for attention. Dabbles of darkening ruby like spray paint on baled hay. Edna loosening hair through her fingers little French loaves tipped off with bitten ragged fingernails. Imperfect aglets upon raveled laces. Shannon fidgeted as often she flew away from Edna's grasp but this touch was the touch she required. The warm flesh of hair like water shearing. Veil or boat's remnant wake and then rebraided deftly again all Edna's handiwork and she was a studied expert having at one point braided every child's hair in Palmyra all her friends' children and all her schoolgirl companions.

What do you think she asked Shannon holding the end of her hair around for the girl to see. Shannon fiddled it between her thumbs. Oh I think it's getting along. Are you thinking about things Shannon. Well duh. Silence for a while. The attic heat oppressive and light shifting behind the glass.

Edna whispered I'm glad you live here and Shannon shrugged it seemed all the time like everyone wanted her to cover their loneliness. I'm a whole lotta trouble ma'am she said nothing but trouble for you and Edna clucked her tongue no no no trouble at all dear I always wanted a girl of my own and I guess if I'd had a daughter she'd be only a little younger than you now. You mean if you'd had one with the Father. Edna didn't answer for a while then argued it could've been anybody. But it wasn't anybody she said. No it wasn't you're right. Let's stop talking about him he's a dung beetle nobody. What exactly do you mean by that dear. I just don't wanna talk about him during you-and-me times.

You-and-me times.

Yeah you-and-me times like now with you braiding my hair even though I'm gonna mess it up first thing when you finish and you know it.

You-and-me times Edna repeated fascinating the syllables in her mouth you-and-me times the precious candlestick of flare and dwelling together. Well what should we talk about then. Shannon laughed her throat scabby calloused summer palms. Did you know she said not all dung beetles roll it some bury it. It. Shit. Oh dear. She laughed her tunnelling laugh again back of her head on Edna's breast holy illumination on Edna's yellow shirt her lovely flaxen hair twisted at the temples and she brushed it away behind her ears and kissed her sweaty forehead before the girl could get away. You don't know where I been Shannon chided all over creation and in the dirt and then some. If you make me sick started Edna and left it at that. Just left it.

Tell me a fact ma'am. A fact. Yessim some sorta fact you know like what I know about dung beetles and shit. Hm well you know how our flowers are pinkish out front of the house. I know it. Do you know why we want them pink and plant so many of those flowers around Palmyra they're called hydrangeas. Why. If the flowers are pink it's good corn and soy soil they'll turn blue if there's too much acid in the ground. What really. Really we'll cut some tomorrow and I'll show you in a vase. Is that really how you tell what grows good. In the old days I'm sure nowadays they have science to tell them but I always liked the flower way. I think I like it too.

About to say don't change Shannon don't ever change it nearly tripped from her love-drunk tongue but then thought twice. Did the girl even have a choice. Of course she would change and of course she wouldn't. And what did it matter to Edna after all so long as Shannon was here with her now reeking to high heaven of blood and urine and bugs a long braid continuing its slow progress down molehills of her spine and another summer morning rising its rosy breath into the perfect plaits of her hair.

And that night in bed the Father would have the dream only this time the Coroner turned with him and he felt good arms helping his ribs calmly rise and lower with impossible air.

When he woke the Coroner was watching him a slant of light
from the window putting gold under his eyelids. Were you dreaming.
I was I had a dream again it's not the first time I've had it I wish I was
like Daniel I could tell you what it was about but sometimes it's hard
enough remembering what all happened. If you remember anything
tell me. It feels like so much and so little all at once in my dream I'm
sleeping in the sun and while my eyes are closed god creates everything
only this time I heard it.

The Coroner asked what did you hear.

The one word he used to speak me alive it startled me so I woke
up and saw you lying here and I knew nothing in my life would be sad
again and if it was sad it would also be good I saw everything and it was
good. Do you remember what the word was. I cannot say what it was I
promised not to tell.

In the morning coming from bed slowly. Told the Coroner he loved
him again and had no reservations about it saw behind his head the
window a rectangular blue tag with some trees coming up through to
pull back the paper. Oh and it was beautiful. Touched the Coroner's
side parallel to his own ribs his good and pleasant flesh and firmness
underneath some structure holding him up holding him there that was
beautiful too. For a while he stilly lay pressed with his ear against the
Coroner's throat heard his heart flapping open and shut and that was
equally beautiful as everything. He felt deeply the living and dead he
allowed himself to feel it deep the living and dead and alive again and
so for the first time he knew what the idea of his god might feel like.
He might feel like this. He might feel like a neck when you are lucky
enough to be close and hear it really making a life. He might speak
through blood and live in you quietly preparing a room. It might not
be easy work it might be so difficult all by himself until one day.

Made coffee. Sat drinking it at the dining table. Troubled about
Shannon. The Coroner caught him staring out at nothing and smiled
what are you thinking right now. The Father shook his head. Shannon

Wells I have to speak to her as soon as I can before I forget. Forget what. Forget whatever joy is in me now I think it's best if I speak to everyone while I still remember it. He washed out his mug went to blue farmhouse across the street wearing just his sweatpants and sleepshirt. Knocked on the door and it was Shannon who answered with a braid in her hair. Come talk with me by the lake he said okay and they went together to walk the perimeter of the lake following the thread tight between them.

I think it's about time I have a generally serious talk with you and not like usual like we're the same age and friends or anything but as if I were really your father and had something to teach you and also something to confess to you. A stern look from her the one he was afraid of receiving and she nodded. I know what it's like to be in your position and I'm sorry I can't help but feel I've caused this pain for you. Why's that. Because I died first and came back first. Is that why you left town and left Edna. No but it was a contributing factor to both those things for sure from the start I contained certain unchristian predilections and I thought it best that I remain lonely for the rest of my life. That's stupid. I know that now and I wish I'd known it sooner.

You died she said then he repeated I died. Okay that's something I suspected anyway. How did you suspect it. Well for one you're very sad. For two. For two I know you. Do you really. Maybe but maybe it don't really matter because one day I will and you'll know me too everyone will be there. I don't know I'm still scared. That's okay too.

How's your side. She lifted the edge of her shirt said see for yourself man. A little puckered white hem fresh after her ribs stopped beside her belly button. Your Coroner did a good job on me I think and I got a pretty cool scar too. Are you going to show Ian. No I don't think I will but maybe I'll show Edna. Where'd you get a gun. I ain't going to tell you that part but I'll tell you what.

What.

So what if this was the place. If this was the place then everything would be alright but it wouldn't be alright for long and then it wouldn't be alright for a while again but it would be alright. Shannon he said I love you too and he meant it but it was complicated wasn't it how many people he could love and still not feel full up from the loving or secure at all he felt this shift inside him. He felt a cataclysmic tearing.

When he was younger he remembered his Old Father and mother standing at the shore of the lake holding both his arms swinging until his arc reached its terminal zenith and releasing him then he flew into the lake and broke the waves with his body and in those brief moments when no one held him he experienced absolute rapture. But in his adolescent years he felt the earth rocking him with those same motions he recalled the initial dread taking hold as strange strength heaved him away from the familiar crushed grass underfoot dizzy swinging eyes the frightening slip of hands out of hands. Upon release he grew older as he fell hanging himself on the wire meant to connect him to all mankind.

As he watched Shannon Wells she went away from him a little tread slow the bank and slipped herself under the water.

She closed her eyes. Oil. At the beginning of the world she remembered the tang of oil. A crowded black bolt knit up by all those who loved her covering her and there was no throwing it off now never nor ever. She knew no one died really. There were the other people who'd carry her life around it was heavy and invisible and totally insoluble as stones in the gall of their blood it was burden it was toil it was misery it was longing it was love great irredeemable redoubling love for her for all creation and people for a place where they knew the names of each molecule of soil. She would miss them if she were dead but she wouldn't die. No one died in Palmyra Ohio.

From now on the days would be shorter the shadows shorter too during trim evenings spent in blue isolation winter cold swaddling of beings in their own skeletons. No more gnats over ears damp coolness washed over tops of feet dust motes materialized in heat sparrows magnetized to tops of trees and fields and bushes now horizons turn navy and lavender molecules of water rise from the earth and solidify into a crust broken by boot prints for shoveling first would come a small golden period. Then sleep. If I could pull the sun down to you. If I could hold it in your heart. Oh man he says. The quality of light there is different. In the evening it comes down in a pink gold wash. A man locked out of his fishing shed trying to break into it with rebar and a doorstop he doesn't know where the light comes from a woman watching the bees move doesn't know either not the girl crouched in the grass pulling petals off weeds not the Coroner feeding the Father's chickens quiet and sure of posture and who does but the Father likes to think now he does and what he knows commands him. Move. Oh man he says oh you wonder at what is good when the word points back to you. Has always.

ACKNOWLEDGEMENTS

I'm grateful for the friends and family who offered to read Palmyra (and other works of mine) before I sent it out to What Books—Kyle Cochrun, Julia Coursen, Regina Rudder, Sarah Kabacinski-Willis, Stephanie Serna, Michael Rodden, and Kennedy King. For your support and love and wisdom: thank you. Sorry if I've forgotten anybody.

I have so much gratitude for Kate Haake and the incredible What Books Press team for the support and labor and care it took to bring this project to life. I couldn't have asked for more, especially as a first-time novelist. It felt truly kismet.

For the town of Mount Vernon, Ohio, and Mount Vernon Nazarene University, for being places I called home for a while.

And most of all, I'm unendingly grateful to the poet John Ballenger. Thanks for teaching me, and for your friendship. This is for you.

HENRY ELIZABETH CHRISTOPHER is a trans writer living in Seattle, Washington. His writing has been published in journals such as *The Threepenny Review*, *Little Patuxent Review*, *Gordon Square Review*, *Delay Fiction*, *HASH*, *Gigantic Sequins* and *Eastern Iowa Review*. He's received nominations for both the Pushcart Prize and Best of the Net and is working toward his MFA in Fiction with the University of Washington.

LOS ANGELES

2022

No One Dies in Palmyra Ohio
HENRY ELIZABETH CHRISTOPHER

Us Clumsy Gods
ASH GOOD

Skeletal Lights From Afar
FORREST ROTH

That Blue Trickster Time
AMY UYEMATSU

2021

Pyre
MAUREEN ALSOP

What Falls Away is Always
HAAKE & WRONSKY, EDITORS

The Eight Mile Suspended Carnival
REBECCA KUDER

Game
M.L. WILLIAMS

2020

No, Don't
ELENA KARINA BYRNE

One Strange Country
STELLA HAYES

Remembering Dismembrance:
A Critical Compendium
DANIEL TAKESHI KRAUSE

Keeping Tahoe Blue
ANDREW TONKAVICH

2019

Time Crunch
CATHY COLMAN

Whole Night Through
L.I. HENLEY

Echo Under Story
KATHERINE SILVER

Decoding Sparrows
MARIANO ZARO

2018

Interrupted by the Sea
PAUL LIEBER

The Headwaters of Nirvana
BILL MOHR

2017

Gary Oldman Is a Building
You Must Walk Through
FORREST ROTH

Rhombus and Oval
JESSICA SEQUEIRA

Imperfect Pastorals
GAIL WRONSKY

2016

The Mysterious Islands
A.W. DEANNUNTIS

The "She" Series:
A Venice Correspondence
HOLADAY MASON & SARAH MACLAY

Mirage Industries
CAROLIE PARKER

2015

The Balloon Containing the Water
Containing the Narrative Begins Leaking
RICH IVES

The Shortest Farewells Are the Best
CHUCK ROSENTHAL & GAIL WRONSKY

As a small, independent press, we urge our readers to support
independent booksellers. This is easily done on our website by
purchasing our books either through Indiebound or from BookShop.

WHATBOOKSPRESS.COM